Thomas C. (Thomas Coffin) Amory

Class Memoir of George Washington Warren

With English and American Ancestry

Thomas C. (Thomas Coffin) Amory

Class Memoir of George Washington Warren
With English and American Ancestry

ISBN/EAN: 9783337178987

Printed in Europe, USA, Canada, Australia, Japan

Cover: Foto ©Raphael Reischuk / pixelio.de

More available books at **www.hansebooks.com**

OF

GEORGE WASHINGTON WARREN

WITH

ENGLISH AND AMERICAN ANCESTRY

BY HIS CLASSMATE

THOMAS C. AMORY

TOGETHER WITH

LETTERS, VALEDICTORY POEM, ODES, ETC.

———————

BOSTON

1886

PREFACE.

NO more fitting monument can be raised by filial affection
to a parent's worth than the record of a well-spent life.
Where that life has been a golden tissue of honorable
achievements in public and official duty, of earnest and eloquent utterance in law and letters, in forensic arguments or
popular appeals, marked throughout its several stages by brilliant correspondence and compositions in prose and verse,
which other generations will value, some such record becomes
a sacred obligation. The memoir of Judge Warren, prepared
for his class-book at Harvard, and reprinted in this volume, is a
succinct account of his earthly career. It might have been
indefinitely extended to embrace all in its course that was
memorable, — the history of the period in which he took so
conspicuous a part; but that would not have been consistent
with the object of that publication, or of this.

We should have been glad to have embraced here, likewise, a
large selection from his printed works. It is hoped this may be
accomplished later, perhaps in another volume. The opportunity, however, is improved to present a few selections in verse,
and the very admirable letters of his father, Mr. Isaac Warren,
addressed to him, from his school days to his early manhood.

His correspondence with other members of his family, with
friends, and many of his eminent cotemporaries with whom he
interchanged letters on subjects of importance, and much else
likely to perish if not so preserved, would tell better than any
bare recital of events his claim to be remembered.

It had also been intended to append to this memoir an engraving of its subject; but circumstances beyond control have compelled this, also, to be deferred.   In the Lodge at Bunker Hill is a bust of the judge, taken by Dexter in 1857, and presented by request, after his death, by his son, Gen. Lucius H. Warren, to the Association over which he so long presided.   It was said to have been at that time a faithful portrait.   It is intended to have engraved the very excellent painting in oil of Mr. Isaac Warren, now belonging also to this son of the judge, in his house in Philadelphia.   As that son is soon to take his departure on Ariel's flit around the globe, this also must await his return.

T. C. A.

NAHANT, August 4, 1886.

CONTENTS.

MEMORIAL

OF

GEORGE WASHINGTON WARREN.

1813 — 1883.

G EORGE WASHINGTON WARREN, son of Isaac
Warren and Abigail Fiske, was born in Charlestown,
now part of the city of Boston, October 1, 1813. He
died in that city, in the house next west of the Boston Athe-
næum, May 13, 1883.

That the first American progenitor of this name was like
Macænas, as Horace relates in the first line of the Odes, *atavis
editus regibus*, — a very common privilege, if any it be, — has
been made clear by the work of Doctor John C. Warren upon
the descendants of Gundreda. It seems more than probable
that his ancestor, John, who came over to Massachusetts in
1630, with Winthrop and Saltonstall, was brother of Richard of
Plymouth, and the father of Peter, from whom the author of
that work traces his descent. That John, the ancestor of the
Warrens of Watertown, was identical with the companion of
Saltonstall, seems difficult to doubt. We reserve for a more
fitting occasion the grounds of this belief; not that they are
without interest here, where the name and blood of the Warrens are so largely represented, but for the reason that this
memoir of our classmate already occupies so many pages.

In the sixth generation from this John (1585–1667), who
settled at Watertown, on Massachusetts Bay, in 1630, his
ascending line of ancestry are: Isaac, 1758–1834; Elisha, 1716–

1795; John, 1684–1745; John, 1665–1703; Daniel. All of them appear to have possessed the sterling qualities to win from their contemporaries affection and respect. Their memories, kept in mind by many a monument of their own achievement, are still cherished by their descendants as their most precious heirloom. They in turn inherited and transmitted that good sense, integrity, and thrift which secured to them, as their generations moved on, health and happiness, the confidence of the public, with a fair share of official responsibilities and honors. The trust in Providence, which insured them independence, and in so many ways constituted life a blessing, is observable in what we know of their experiences and in the correspondence they have left.

George's father had already been twice a widower when, in 1810, he married Abigail Fiske, the widow of Isaac Lamson, of Weston, who was born April 4, 1769, and died 1858, at the advanced age of eighty-nine. We find frequent intermarriages between the Warrens, Lamsons, and Fiskes, — families all alike honored and honorable in their various branches. The Fiskes were especially distinguished as divines in the Puritan pulpit, as able expounders and eloquent preachers. The Warrens may have been somewhat more independent in their religious belief. We find that John, the original patriarch, who had settled at Watertown, had acquired there a large estate. He served as selectman from 1636 to 1640. When Endicott ruled the colony, 1651–1661, he was proceeded against for expressing his dissent, not long before he died, to portions of the Cambridge platform. His descendants were generally, however, steadfast to the faith of their fathers, and George's parents, rigid Calvinists, would have been pleased if their son, the subject of this memoir, had kept true to the ancestral belief.

When eight years of age, in 1821, he was sent to board with Rev. Mr. Webster, at Hampton, on the southern borders of New Hampshire, that he might attend the Academy at that place. Here he remained two years. From the summer of 1823 to the summer of 1824 he was at the Framingham Academy, and the next year at that of Stowe, where he met his future wife, a scholar at the same school. Such opportunities for studying the marvels of nature at the period of life when the mind and imagination are peculiarly sensitive to their impressions were not thrown away on one so happily constituted. His teachers were of the best to inspire a taste for knowledge, to quicken his mental faculties, as also to develop his sense of right.

The letters of his father, still extant, and which he often reperused as he progressed, were admirably calculated to form his character upon elevated standards, to instil principles of religious responsibility and dependence, which he exemplified in his character and conduct throughout the vicissitudes of his life. In selecting Amherst for his collegiate course his father may have in some measure been actuated by one of his wife's brothers having been connected with that institution as a professor; he also cherished the hope that the influences of the place might dispose George to follow in the footsteps of so many of his progenitors and become a Puritan minister. Another brother of Mrs. Warren, Dr. Thaddeus Fiske, was settled over the parish of West Cambridge, now Arlington, for half a century. He was himself a deacon in the First Church of Charlestown, of which Dr. Morse, the geographer, was pastor. By nature and nurture preëminently religious and devout, the concerns of this life were less precious in his sight than those of that to come.

To a young lad of twelve, of an ardent temperament, jealous of restraint, with special aptitude for enjoyment, such a future as that his father in the goodness of his heart had planned for him was peculiarly distasteful. The gloomy austerities of Amherst soon became repugnant to all his conceptions of what was pleasant and agreeable. He had not been long within its walls before his forebodings were more than realized. Displeased and discontented he besought his father with respectful firmness to remove him to Harvard, where his surroundings would be more congenial. The parental decision, that he better remain where he was, he obeyed, and with filial affection and reverence he submitted even with a good grace to what he could not control. He frequently afterwards, in all frankness, returned to the subject in his correspondence and conversation,

and to one whose pains had been untiring to form his mind and
character it must have pleased the father to see this mark of
independence in stating fearlessly his reasons for the faith that
was in him.

He had been nearly two years at Amherst when an incident
occurred, somewhat distressing to them both at the time, to set
him free. One day, emptying a bowl of water from his window
down upon the footpath underneath, some drops sprinkled the
dress of a member of the faculty who was passing, too much
absorbed in his meditations to take heed of any such possibility
of peril. It may have been unintentional. There seems, however, to have been some suspicion that it was from design, and
to resent some supposed injustice. It ruffled the temper of the
don, who reported the misdemeanor, though Mr. Warren and
his friends endeavored to avert the consequences as out of proportion to the offence. The government of the college, in-
censed at this presumed indignity to one of their august body,
were not to be appeased. George was suspended.

It seems to have been his good fortune to pursue his studies
under favorable conditions for diligence and in pleasant places,
where nature presented to his plastic spirit in the scenery and
cultivation about him much both to charm and instruct. In
charge of the Rev. Dr. Stowe, of Braintree, he worked with
little interruption, and in 1827, well fitted for his examination, he
became at last, as he had so long eagerly desired, a student of
Harvard. He entered the Sophomore class, and, though he had
only attained his fourteenth year, his own experience, the instructions of many cultivated minds, eager for his own sake and
his father's to quicken his mind and discipline his character,
had not been in vain.

His diligence within the college walls at Cambridge continued
unabated, and though the youngest of his classmates, and
many of them very much older than himself and more mature,
he ranked well for scholarship. He gained and kept the
respect of the professors and teachers, formed many lasting
friendships with his classmates and with those in the classes
above and below, and was generally beloved. For the Hasty
Pudding Society he wrote a poem in 1829, and in 1830, chosen

class poet, another for that occasion, which, well conceived and happily phrased, deserved and elicited applause.

In the winter vacation of the year that he graduated, as was then not unusual where such opportunities offered, he was an assistant teacher of the Warren Academy at Woburn, which his father had recently founded. His father had not abandoned the hope, now that he had obtained his degree, that he would carry out the plan still fondly cherished, and become an Ortho-dox minister. But, when he urged upon him the study of divinity, he found to his grief that George had conscientious scruples, having become sceptical as to the Westminster Cate-chism and Cambridge platform. What he had apprehended from the influences of Harvard, and which had led to his pref-erence for Amherst, had come to pass, for his son had become a Unitarian. He was too firmly fixed in his own religious views not to be disappointed, too sincere a Christian himself to disturb the faith of another. This disappointment did not lessen their cordial affection, and they remained good friends as before.

This inability to carry out his father's plan for him had one good effect. He felt it all the more incumbent upon him to be permanently pecuniarily independent of his father, and he accepted an offer made to him to become assistant teacher in the Friends' Academy at New Bedford. The next year he opened, under his own tuition, a classical school for young ladies, which continued until 1834. Coming fresh from the instruction of Harvard, which, if not as varied and complete as at present, made many excellent scholars, with his harness on, his mind well furnished, his æsthetic nature vivid with his own considerable experiences in life and extended scholarship, he was well constituted to inspire the young ladies intrusted to his charge with a thirst for knowledge. By making instruction pleasant he sought not only to develop and regulate their facul-ties, but to fix tenaciously in their memories what it was good for them to know. He took especial pains to render his school-rooms cheerful and attractive, and his cordial and sym-pathetic disposition, while ever chastened by his high sense of obligation and the importance of maintaining his authority, in-spired friendship and confidence.

His varied accomplishments in letters eminently fitted him for his task. Besides being well grounded in the classics he spoke French, Spanish, and Italian. He was well acquainted with the masterpieces of those languages, and was in the habit of reading weekly, up to the day of his death, his Hebrew Bible and the Greek Testament. If the instruction of Harvard was not so universal as now, many branches of knowledge, such as metaphysics and mathematics, were then less abstruse and remote. What was needed for the general purposes of life was more simply inculcated and better understood, for it was less entangled with subtle distinctions and puzzling limitations. If dialectics are more scientific, the more certain knowledge derived from intuition and observation as taught by Locke, by Stuart, Reed, and Browne, whose works we then studied, of the operations of the human mind and our moral and emotional nature, was quite as valuable as our present doubts.

This pleasant relation of instructor to the best and brightest of the choicest circles of New Bedford opened wide to him the gates of its society, one eminently refined and cultivated. He became a great favorite with those most eminent in professional walks. Many already known over the land, or who have since become distinguished, were among his intimate associates. It is sufficient to mention the Hon. Thomas Dawes Eliot, Governor John H. Clifford, Judge Oliver Prescott, Benjamin Rotch, and Benjamin Lindsay. Their very names explain why his residence in this beautiful city of gardens he ever afterwards remembered as one of the happiest periods of his life.

His correspondence even from the time he entered college and down to this period, when he had reached his majority, shows how desirous he was of passing his life in the pursuits of literature and of becoming an author or professor. While at New Bedford he was tendered the position of tutor at Amherst College, which he declined, and afterwards, when he was offered a similar position at Harvard, his father would not let him accept it. He delivered a lecture before the Lyceum of New Bedford, and wrote an ode for the Fourth of July of the same year, which was afterward set to music and sung in Boston on a similar occasion (1881), when he was the orator.

His father had watched tenderly over his progress, and by his constant letters from his early childhood to one of his latest from his death-bed manifested his profound affection. These letters, and those of his son in reply to them, were religiously preserved and read over again when he had his own children to direct in the ways of wisdom and discretion. They would occupy too large a space for this memoir. When, as intended, they are made accessible in print, the happy influence they exerted in forming the character of the son will be recognized. His father died at Charlestown, March 19, 1834, at the ripe age of seventy-six, as George was reaching his majority.

Thus cast upon his own resources, with a slender patrimony, George decided to adopt the law for his profession, and came to it with a training and ability, matured in other pursuits, that ensured a successful career. He entered the office of Mr. Benjamin Rand and Augustus H. Fiske, his cousin, at the corner of Court and Washington streets, in Boston. Mr. Rand ranked among the most learned of the Suffolk bar. In several departments of the law he was preëminent, and from his familiarity with that of insurance had been retained with Mr. William Wirt, who had come on from Baltimore for the purpose, against Mr. Webster in the well-known case of Tuttle Hubbard and Brooks, tried in the old Court-house, afterwards the City Hall, which stood on the site of the present. His ability and learning displayed in the case were so conspicuous that he sprang at once from comparative obscurity to an elevated position in his profession. Fees flowed in from cases in which large sums were at stake, and with Mr. Fiske, a most successful practitioner, for his partner, though the two were very differently constituted, they amassed each a handsome fortune. Mr. Rand when in London was made much of by the judges and lawyers, honored and feasted, for they realized his worth even better than his own legal brotherhood.

He possessed one of the best law libraries in Boston. Its well-stocked shelves lining his chambers on two floors, connected by an iron circular stair, were an education. Their precious stores of legal learning, their possessor, of whose heart they were almost the exclusive object of affection and pride, had for years been absorbing, till he cared little for aught else. He was too honest to neglect the obligation assumed in taking pupils, and, generally shy and taciturn in general conversation, he was all the more ready to communicate his treasures when prompted by the sense of duty, and his students were interested and sensible. It is easy to conceive how valuable these lessons must have proved, for Warren, during his long period of practice at the bar or later when seated on the bench. Nor had he less happily selected the office for the details of professional practice. Its docket was large and varied. Mr. Fiske, his cousin, the partner of Mr. Rand, stood among the first in office routine and management of cases in court, and left him little to learn from his own stumbles.

Attachment to Harvard, that prompted its choice for his *alma mater*, did not abate as he advanced in years. He was a constant attendant at commencements, and at class-meetings helped to keep alive and fervid the good-fellowship that subsisted. All of us remember that pleasant gathering seven years ago at his own house on Marlboro' street, when most of our survivors were clustered round the hospitable banquet he had prepared for us. Late into the summer night we discoursed college days and incidents, renewing our youth in their pleasant memories. We have had other meetings that were memorable. If more are vouchsafed in the somewhat precarious future for some of us our host on that occasion will never be forgotten.

One year before our classmate entered the bar he studied at Cambridge in the then new law school, of which Justice Story and Mr. Greenleaf were professors and Charles Sumner, his classmate, a tutor and librarian. No examination was then required, and, after the period specified for his preparation, the training was completed, he took his oaths and was admitted to the bar. He opened a law office in Charlestown, was engaged in a number of important causes in Middlesex county, and subsequently, with Mr. George Farrar, as Warren & Farrar, had a large practice.

He had been married April 30, 1835, by Rev. Joseph Bennett, of Woburn, to Lucy Rogers Newell, a daughter of Dr. Jonathan Newell, of Stowe, who had been his schoolmate in the academy of that place. She was a grand-daughter of a distinguished divine of the same name, who held liberal views of theology, and a descendant of the martyr, John Rogers. She was born August 15, 1813, and consequently was but four months younger than himself. Their union soon ended in her death, Sept. 4, 1840. The only child of this marriage was Gen. Lucius H. Warren, born Oct. 6, 1838, who served during our civil war with great honor, and who now resides in Philadelphia practising law.

George did not remain long a widower, for on the first of June of the succeeding year he was married by Rev. George E. Ellis, D.D., to Georgiana Thompson, daughter of Joseph and Susan Pratt Thompson, of Charlestown, who survives him. Her mother was the daughter of Capt. John Pratt, an eminent merchant of Boston. Thus happy in his home and his social connections, generally beloved and esteemed in the community around him, his practice rapidly extended, and at the same time tokens of the confidence reposed in his ability and character followed in rapid succession. On April 14, 1837, he had been appointed Justice of the Peace, and Jan. 6, 1840, Master in Chancery.

In 1844 and 1845 he served in the Legislature, and was the Whig candidate for Congress in 1846. He was instrumental in obtaining the city charter for Charlestown, and was elected first mayor under it in 1847, and reëlected for three additional terms. When elected mayor he was but thirty-four, and younger than any other member of the City Council. Untiring in his attention to the improvements of the city, and particularly of the public schools, he took an active part in the building of new school-houses, as also in the establishment of the High School. He delivered the address at laying the corner-stone of the latter institution in September, 1847.

Elected to the Senate in 1853 and 1854, and chairman of the Judiciary Committee, he was the author of the bill to separate the government of Harvard College from that of the State, which passed the Senate in 1854, but failed in the House. It subsequently became a law with immaterial amendments. This act took the election of the Board of Overseers out of the

control of the Legislature and placed it in the hands of the
alumni of three years' standing. He carried through the Legislature the bill for the annexation of Charlestown to Boston,
which was accepted by the vote of the citizens of both cities in
October, 1854, but was set aside by the Supreme Court. He
subsequently agitated the question until it was finally accomplished in 1872.

In his political faith and affiliation he was steadfastly con-
servative. In 1844 he was sent delegate as a Webster Whig to
the convention in Philadelphia which nominated Henry Clay
for the presidency when Polk was elected. In June, 1852,
again delegate to the convention at Baltimore, he labored with
Rufus Choate for the nomination of Webster. Scott was the
successful candidate of the convention, and Pierce was chosen
President. In 1856 he was sent to the convention at the same
place, where Fillmore was nominated by the Whigs, Fremont
by the Republicans, and when Buchanan was elected by the
Democrats. He soon after withdrew from politics, and spent a
year in Europe. Upon his return from abroad he opened his
law office in Boston, and soon had his share of clients.

Still hoping that the country might be saved from the civil
war impending, he did what he could with lip and pen to soothe
the angry spirit of animosity that raged between the sections.
This was not then the popular side in Boston, though many of
the more sensible, who knew what civil war signified, and how
great might be its wreck, preferred to join the Democrats than
be faithless to the obligations of the Constitution. In that
momentous election of 1860, when Lincoln was chosen, Warren
cast his vote for Breckenridge. When the South took up arms
he rallied to the support of the government, and voted with
the Republicans. He was at this time the candidate on that
ticket for Attorney-General of the State.

Although many of the great luminaries that had shed lustre
on the Suffolk bar and attained historical importance had dis-
appeared from view or shone in other spheres, enough remained
for emulation. But with his studious tastes, and other aptitudes
for the bench, his selection, April 12, 1862, for the position of
Judge of the Municipal Court of Charlestown, with its varied

jurisdiction, civil and criminal, was eminently fortunate. His long experience at the bar, his familiar acquaintance with the people under his jurisdiction, his amiable and cheerful disposition, his courteous and dignified deportment to all, his conscientiousness, his quick intuitions and insight into motive, his freedom from prejudice, his readiness in the application of rules and principles, his firmness, patience, and impartiality, well fitted him for that bench or any other, and for twenty-one years that he held the office he gave no reason to complain to counsel, the public, or even to a disappointed suitor.

If somewhat mysterious in their ways to the uninitiated, Freemasonry, judged by the character of its members, has every claim to respect and confidence. Judge Warren, Oct. 9, 1843, had been made a Mason in King Solomon's Lodge, which had buried Gen. Joseph Warren, killed at Bunker Hill in 1775. He took the Knight Templar's and Thirty-third degree, and became a member of the De Molay Encampment. Through his exertions the Henry Price Lodge was established in 1858. Of this he was the first Master for two years, and in 1861 was Deputy Grand Master of the Grand Lodge, and during the absence of the Grand Master at the South filled his place.

He had been a Director of the Bunker Hill Association from 1836 to 1839, and its Secretary from 1839 to 1847. June 24, 1845, he delivered the Masonic address, upon the Monument grounds, upon the occasion of placing the model of the original monument, erected by King Solomon's Lodge in memory of Joseph Warren seventy years before, inside the present noble obelisk. In 1847 he was chosen President, and continued by annual elections to 1875 for twenty-eight years, and then again chosen Director, he remained till his decease in 1883, seven years longer.

Having been made a member of this Association by his father, at the age of eleven, he was connected with it for nearly fifty-nine years. During that period a number of historical incidents occurred, in which he was a prominent actor. As a boy he attended the laying the corner-stone of the Monument. When he became Secretary the obelisk was only eighty feet high, and he was the leading spirit in the movement for the

Ladies' Monument Fair of 1840, which brought about its successful completion. He was a member of the committee which had charge of the celebration of its completion, in 1843, — the grandest celebration which had taken place in this country up to that date. During his presidency four important celebrations occurred, — first, in 1850, on the seventy-fifth anniversary; second, in 1857, at the inauguration of the statue of Gen. Joseph Warren; third, in 1861, at the great flag-raising from the apex of the Monument, just after the opening of the war; and fourth, in 1875, at the Centennial celebration, — on all of which occasions he presided and made addresses. On Oct. 19, 1860, he received the Prince of Wales and suite, upon the occasion of their visit to the historic grounds, and, the following year, Prince Napoleon. He was the first to establish the custom of patriotic hospitality. People of note who visited the historic Monument were brought there through his efforts, and were handsomely entertained at his hospitable mansion, which, at that time, was situated on Monument square. At the annual celebrations of the battle his home was usually thronged with visitors from all parts of the country.

Nor should it be forgotten that, after his declination to serve longer as President, he assisted at another most memorable occasion connected with the Monument. When, on the somewhat tardy recognition of the claims of Prescott to be held in remembrance, the admirable statue, by Story, was erected on the hill; he was present as one of the Board of Directors of the Association at its consecration. The Honorable Robert C. Winthrop delivered an eloquent address, fitting to the place and its memories, — a brilliant audience hanging with rapt attention on his lips, which never disappointed expectation on a great historic theme. How many of those that were present that beautiful day, under the canopy of heaven, who had listened to the trumpet tones of Webster and the siren syllables of Everett on that consecrated ground, at the earlier commemorations, have since ceased to exist!

If not a descendant, or even near relation, of the great proto-martyr whose name he bore, he had an hereditary interest in the strike for independence. His father was a soldier of the Revolution, though not at Bunker Hill. There is now in the possession of his grandson, Gen. Lucius H. Warren, a piece of blue ribbon enclosed in a letter, which reads as follows: " Fifty years after the memorable battle of Lexington, at the anniversary at Concord, this ribbon was worn as a badge of distinction by those who were under arms and fought in defence of their country against the British troops on that eventful day. This is to be kept by my son or grandson so long as there is one left of my heirs." This letter is addressed to George Washington Warren or Isaac Henry Warren.

Ever foremost in advocating improvements for his native city he was the originator of the Charlestown Gas Company, and its first President. Its establishment met with great opposition from the large majority of the citizens who considered that the introduction of gas would be a great injury. He was one of the fathers and directors of the Charlestown Branch Railroad Company, now the Fitchburg, and also of the Lexington and West Cambridge.

He was a trustee of the Warren Institution for Savings for forty-four years; and for nearly forty-three a trustee — thirty-three of which he was President — of the Warren Academy, at Woburn, Mass., which institution was founded by his father. He was also President of the Massachusetts Colonization Society, and for many years a delegate to American Colonization Society, at the annual meetings in Washington. For many years he was an active member of the Board of Trustees of Donations for Education in Liberia, and a zealous and eloquent advocate of the Republic of Liberia, in the promotion of whose interests he was specially engaged almost to the last hours of his active and philanthropic life. It was mainly by his efforts the petition was gotten up by the citizens, which secured from the Legislature the act authorizing the systems of parks around Boston which is now being carried out.

The Christian principles inculcated by his father grew with his growth, and though unable to accept the extreme view of the Orthodox, in the Harvard Church at Charlestown, under the ministry of Dr. James Walker, the President of Harvard, later of Dr. George E. Ellis, he displayed throughout his life the benign influence of his faith in his walk and conversation. When he removed to the Back Bay he became a prominent member of the First Church, under Dr. Rufus E. Ellis, who preached his funeral discourse. He was a delegate to the Unitarian Conference from its first meeting.

His interest in the history of his own country never flagged. At the meetings of the New England Historical and Genealogical Society, and of the Bostonian, established to preserve and care for the Old State-House, he was a most constant attendant, and often spoke. He was a member of the Royal Historical Society of London, a delegate to the Peace Conference at Liverpool in 1882. Among other numerous societies of which he was a member may be mentioned the Woman's Club, the Suffolk Bar Association, and the Thursday Evening or Warren Club, of which President Wm. B. Rogers was president, to the literary entertainment of which he often contributed in prose and verse. In these and in all other social relations he was loved and valued. He was the intimate friend of Edward Everett, of Rufus Choate, and Daniel Webster, and at the request of Mr. Webster prepared that part of his Life, which relates to his addresses in laying the corner-stone and completion of the Bunker Hill Monument.

His busy pen left much that will be always precious to those who knew him as well as to the general public. His published works, his correspondence, and what can be rescued from the oblivion of the past, it is proposed to collect with a more minute detail of his busy life. Such a life, honored and useful, crowded with incident, has much to record full of instructions and for example to other generations. It certainly will be of peculiar interest to his surviving classmates, who knew him so well.

We should leave incomplete a singularly well-poised character if we omitted to refer to what has been so often remarked and expressed by those who knew him the best,—his amiable qualities. Frank and generous by nature and discipline, he carried alike into work and recreation their cheer and their charm. In the intercourse of public affairs, in the discharge of judicial functions, in his cheerful equanimity at home and in social companionship, his vigor, animation, and magnetic sympathies, engendered affection. Whatever his sound judgment indicated as best, without self-assertion he took the lead. On the bench his dignified amenity conciliated confidence, inspired deference to authority, held waywardness in check. Parties, counsel, and witnesses, assured of his utter freedom from prejudice, his conscientious regard for their rights, held in higher veneration the judgment-seat. The litigation that came to his tribunal, if not involving the largest amounts in value, came home to the daily concerns of the people. It often excited animosities and ruffled the temper. He was happily constituted to calm the troubled spirits and reconcile disputes.

From the time we left Harvard, throughout his busy career, he was for many of us the constant friend and frequent companion. All who shared his daily walks or watched his progress from distances more remote with less opportunity of meeting, bear witness to the firm and uninterrupted hold he kept on their regard. Higher office fell to the lot of some of his classmates on broader theatres of action than his own. Sumner in the Federal Senate gained a world-wide renown in stirring days affecting the destiny of the nation. Kerr represented his country at a foreign court, sat in the Federal Congress. There, too, Potter, Judge of the Supreme Court of his State, and Worcester, son of the great lexicographer, took their part in the national councils which others of the class, as probably Judge Warren himself, could have shared had their other obligations permitted. Fifteen of his class gained various distinction on the bench or at the bar, nine in the pulpit, five in the art of healing. Several by their productions added works of value to the national literature. All who retained their health showed the influence of Harvard, the mettle of their pasture, by their achievements and example, their character and usefulness, and they all loved Warren. He too left his trace in many official trusts, and in his many publications, one of which, the history of the great monument at Bunker Hill, as the record of its erection and the interpretation of all it commemorates, will be perennial as the obelisk itself. His pen was ever busy, and he wrote much else in verse and prose. With his natural endowments and scholarly attainments, the incidents of his life we have so imperfectly related, with the noble traits that composed his honorable, generous, and estimable character, one *teres rotundus* without flaw or blemish, he needed none of the factitious distinctions of rank or special monument for his memory to be cherished. Not only by us, his friends and associates at Cambridge and in the community to which he made himself in so many ways useful, will he long be held in remembrance; but as an example and encouragement to coming generations, who look to him as their progenitor, or are bound to him in consanguinity, or for other reasons bear him in mind, will what we, who knew him best, have to say of him, be well to have recorded. We have not dwelt upon the sorrows inevitable to human life. Perhaps when we meet, as we may, in other realms of being, we shall learn how unflinchingly he bore his cross, at times even for him a heavy one, up the flinty steps of Calvary. We shall more clearly perceive that to his share of the common lot was in some measure owing the worth that embalmed his memory for them and for us.

Some few of us stood around his open sepulchre ten months ago at Mount Auburn,[1] when his coffin stood open to the blue and cloudless skies of that May afternoon, that we might take a parting look of his genial face before his remains were laid within the ground beside his kinsfolks. When we remembered how well through trial and temptation he had walked on with his sturdy step, blameless to the end, we could understand how well life was worth the living, for one who had tried so hard and so well succeeded in accomplishing the tasks set him by Providence to do, and who thus made the best of his mortal existence in the sight of man and God.

---

[1] His remains now rest within a few steps, if not actually on the ground, where John Warren, the first of his family in this country, had his residence, at the place selected, in 1630, by Sir Richard Saltonstall and George Phillips, whose house is still, perhaps, the only local relic of that period. The silent "City of the Dead" now covers a large portion of the ground where the sanguine colonists expected would grow up a great and closely built town. Here John Warren had for other neighbors, the first American Garfield, from whom the late President was descended, and the direct ancestors of many prominent men in various parts of the Union. His house was near the little pond, in the north-east corner of Mount Auburn. In the town of Weston the father of Judge Warren was born, on the old ancestral property, which still, we believe, remains in the Warren family.

ENGLISH ANCESTRY.

TO be descended from kings is a privilege so common, if not universal, as to cease to be ground for pride. History exhibits so many monsters on the thrones of the ages, so many worthless and weak, the temptations and immunities of such lofty position are so apt to demoralize, that minds well regulated attach little value to such distinctions if any they be. One of the characteristics of our race, in all times and conditions, has been, nevertheless, an interest in our progenitors. We all of us take pleasure in following back the several ancestral lines centring in our own individuality radiating back through the centuries. The worship of their ancestors constituted the religion of nations from the dawn of civilization, and even as they became more enlightened this tendency has kept pace with the improved facilities for gaining information with regard to them.

In proportion as such knowledge extends, as celebrities of periods long past become better understood, even more familiar than our own contemporaries, the satisfaction that they belong to us as progenitors or kinsfolk, though remote, vivifies our interest in the history of the periods in which they lived. The examples to follow, or warnings to avoid, they have left behind them come more home to us that the blood which coursed in their veins still trickles in our own. Those who bear the name of Warren should be grateful to the learned physician whose elaborate researches, through skilled experts abroad and at home, have shed such light upon the annals of their race.

How much of the present position of the English-speaking race well abreast in the march of progress, with the van of civilization, is to be attributed to the Norman conquerors of England may be questioned by other nationalities. But courage and greed, their ambition to excel and love of domination, have little abated, and mark them to-day, as when vikings of the Baltic, ten centuries ago, they raided their neighbors. It is said that Gunnora, daughter of a noble Dane, by marriage with Richard, duke of Normandy, was the great-grandmother of the Conqueror, whose daughter Gundreda became the wife of William, first Earl of Warren. For his share of the spoils in the invasion of England he received 240 lordships, and was created by his royal father-in-law Earl of Surrey.

At Lewes, in Sussex, he built his castle, founded the priory, and there died in 1080. His son succeeded and died in 1138, leaving the third earl, whose only daughter, Isabel, married the youngest son of King Stephen, and then Hameline Plantagenet. Her husbands were earls in her rights, and when the Countess Isabel died, in 1202, her son William succeeded as sixth earl, and, after a diversified experience in civil and military service, died in London, in 1239. John, 1235–1304, followed as the seventh earl. In command at the battle of Sterling, in 1294, he was defeated, not from want of courage or conduct on his part, but from disagreements among the English leaders; and he was again in command when he died. His grandson, John, born in 1287, succeeded as the eighth and last earl, and he, dying in 1347, his inheritance went to his sister, Countess of Arundel, whose husband was a Fitzallan.

The earldom and estates in the third generation passed with Isabel, who died in 1138, to De Blois and Plantagenet. Upon the death of John, in 1347, under Edward III., the estates went to the Fitzallans, the title to the crown. It becomes necessary to trace down the line of the second son of the second earl to discover the next representative in seniority of the house of Warren. To judge from their alliances this younger branch had during their several generations maintained a respectable position in field and court. They doubtless shared, in a diminishing scale as they diverged from the main stem, its social consequence and wealth. Their marriages into families of respectability give reason to presume that they had not become impoverished or less respected.

Reginald, next in succession in the male line, now extinct in the genealogy of the house here and in that by Watson in England, is said to have married Adelia, daughter of Roger de Mowbray. In Burke his wife is stated to have been Alice de Wirmgay. It was his brother William, the third earl, who left no son, and whose daughter Isabel, his heiress, married De Blois and Plantagenet, and carried the estates away from the name of Warren. William, the son of Reginald, intermarried with Alice de Townshend; John, his grandson, Joan de Port; his great-grandson, Sir Edward, married Maude de Nereford. Their son, Sir William, when the eighth earl of Surrey died, in 1347, was with King Edward III. at the siege of Calais. That monarch was neither generous nor just. He annexed to the crown many of the estates of the seventh earl, who, when inquired as to the tenure by which he held them, answered, by his sword. The king did not admit the representative of the house to any share of the inheritance, which seems to have diminished little since bestowed by the Conqueror on his son-in-law.

Sir William had no descendants, but Sir Edward continued the line. His son, Sir John, by his wife, Cicily de Eton, married Margaret Stafford, and succeeded to the manor of Stokeport. The line continued on through Nicholas, whose wife was Agnes de Winnington; Sir Lawrence, who, about 1394, married Margaret Bulkeley; John, born 1414, whose wife was Isabel, daughter of Sir John Stanley of Latham, Knight of the Garter, to Sir Lawrence, who, by Isabel Leigh of Adlington, had William, ancestor of Sir John Borlase Warren, of recent naval celebrity, and to Sir John, who, about 1480, marrying Eleanor Girard, had five sons.

The eldest of these sons married Margaret Leigh of Lime; their second son, John, Margaret Molineaux. Sir Edward, their son, by Ann Davenport had thirteen children, and by Susan Booth eleven. Dying in 1609, there came in this line John, who died in 1621; then Edward, born in 1605, for his strength and stature known as Stag Warren, who died in 1687. His son John was a judge, and died in 1705. The line continued, but, of course, became with each generation more remote from our Warrens.

AMERICAN ANCESTRY.

A BOUT the middle of the last century Sir George Warren, Knight of the Bath, affluent and well connected, applied, but without success, to Parliament to be reinstated in the dignity of the Earl of Warren. He claimed to be the lineal representative of the branch of Poynton, and of the second earl, William, who died in 1138, through his second son, Reginald.

Among the ancestors of this Sir George was Sir Lawrence, who, in 1458, married Isabel, daughter of Robert Leigh, of Adlington, in Cheshire. William, his second son, settled in Caunton, Nottinghamshire, and from him descended Sir John Borlase Warren, whose distinguished naval services in the wars with Napoleon gained him fame and title.

John, the eldest son of Sir Lawrence, died in 1525, and his younger son, George, removed to Headboro, in Devon. He had Christopher, whose son William, by Ann Mable, had a son William, who, by Alice Webb, of Sydenham in that county, had seven children, and from this family came to America two sons, Richard and John, supposed to be the ancestors of the Plymouth Warrens, possibly also of this of Watertown. The eldest son, Robert, was parson of Rame. Thomas, the third, is supposed to have died unmarried; but Richard, the fourth son, who had been a merchant at Greenwich, and married Mrs. Marsh, a widow, came over in the "Mayflower" to Plymouth in 1620, and there died young in 1628.

John, the second son, born about 1585, as he is described as forty-five in 1630. That year he came over with Sir Richard Saltonstall in Winthrop's fleet. What became of him, unless he accompanied Saltonstall to Watertown, then including what is now Waltham, does not appear. Dr. Warren believed him to be the father of Peter, to whom he traced his own descent. Peter was born about 1628, and died in 1704, in Roxbury. He was a merchant and master mariner, rich by trade and by marriage. One of his wives was a sister of the Rev. John Williams, captured at Deerfield by the Indians, and was a member of the wealthy family of that name in Roxbury, where Peter and his descendants resided, — one of his sons having erected, in 1730, the dwelling which gave place to the tasteful and substantial mansion Dr. John Collins Warren erected to the memory of his uncle, General Joseph Warren, killed at Bunker Hill, June 17, 1775.

In Dr. John Collins Warren's genealogy, among the visitations is one of Devon, which mentions Richard of Greenwich, who seems unquestionably the head of the Plymouth branch. John, the second son, brother of Robert, parson of Rame, and of the said Richard, Dr. Warren gives good reason for believing his own ancestor father of Peter of Roxbury. This John was forty-five in 1630. Richard died in 1628; his wife, in 1673; they left seven children.

Savage says he could find no proof of connection between the Plymouth, Boston, and Watertown families. Had he discovered any good grounds for believing any such connection inconsistent with what was known he would have probably stated it. Conjecture is no proof, and in genealogical problems nothing should be taken for granted without evidence; but every hypothesis not manifestly untenable should be tested before abandoned. Such investigations are good exercise for the reasoning powers, and by waiting patiently often new data come to light to render probable theories at first discarded. The connecting links between the European and American lines of our progenitors, so generally lost sight of as new interests and connections occupy successive generations, are considered of more importance now that so many sources of information are made available long out of mind.

It may be that two John Warrens came out in Winthrop's fleet, the father of Peter, and John, the settler at Watertown, who came out with Saltonstall. Little is known of John as the father of Peter, but enough of the latter to suggest that they were one and the same person. When the latter died, in 1667,

he mentions four of his children in his will; but not Peter.
Peter was then established at Roxbury, affluent and influential,
with his own children, while his brothers and sisters may have
been more dependent upon their father.   John, of Watertown,
died at the age of eighty-two, in 1667.   Peter, 1628–1704, had
a son, Joseph, 1663–1729, who by Deborah Williams had
Joseph, 1696–1755, who, by Mary Stevens, who died in 1800,
was the father of Gen. Joseph, and Dr. John, 1753–1815, the
father of Dr. John C. Warren.

If, as suggested, John, the father of Peter and John of
Watertown, may have been identical, and the brother of Richard of Plymouth, a reason may be assigned for his coming out
in 1630, worth a thought.   Richard died in 1628.   If the tidings
of his death had reached his brother, it would have been
natural for him to have joined so many of his neighbors who
came out in Winthrop's fleet to ascertain the situation of the
young family thus bereaved, and render help if needed.   The
eldest of these children, Mary, married, in 1628, Robert Bartlett.
If Richard were born in 1588, that might leave little time for
himself and his daughter to grow up, and for her to be of
age to marry.   But marriages took place so often and so young
that would be no embarrassment.

Whether thus, or any other way, these three branches of the
name were connected may not yet have been ascertained.   There
were other Warrens in New England.   The name in the old
country was by common, diffused along the southern, eastern,
and western shores.   In Ireland, early in the sixteenth century,
a family of great respectability flourished near Dublin, from
which came Sir Peter, who commanded the English fleet at the
first reduction of Louisburg.   When in Boston this Sir Peter
said that he descended from the same Poynton branch as our
Warrens.   In the Warren genealogy are visitations of London,
Hertfordshire, Kent, Middlesex, Gloucestershire, Suffolk, War-
wickshire, and Surrey, besides those of Cheshire and Devon, in
which may be traced the ancestral lines of those best known in
Massachusetts.   In eight centuries so good a name might well
spread over the earth, become like the stars in multitude, and,
be respected, whether rich or poor.

All bearing the name may not be derived from Gundreda. Many surnames now in honor came from the occupations of their early progenitors. Many abound taken from the pursuits of the chase. But there seems abundant reason to believe that all who bear the name here of Warren are offshoots of that ancient and honorable stock that professed to hold their lands by their rusty swords. Their earliest English lineal ancestor, by his generalship at Hastings, helped his royal father-in-law to the realm of England, who, from gratitude or paternal affection, requited his services with a large slice of it.

This is an excellent point to start from. It is no slight privilege to possess historical personages for ancestors, or kindred well conditioned and educated, whose character and career, achievements and refinements, are good for example and inspiration, and occupy our own minds with pleasant associations that constitute so large a portion of human happiness.

GENEALOGY.

WARREN.

[Extracts from Bond's History and Genealogy of Watertown.]

1. John Warren, came from England in 1630; age 45; died Dec. 13, 1667.

2. Daniel Warren, 3d child of John Warren; born 1628; took oath 1652.

3. John Warren, 7th child of Daniel Warren; born March, 1665; 1690, "Ensign"; married March 22, 1682; died July 11, 1703.

4. John Warren, son of John Warren; born March 15, 1684; died March 25, 1745; "Deacon"; married Abigail Lamson, June 2, 1708, 2d wife.

5. Elisha Warren, 7th child of John Warren and Abigail Lamson; born April 9, 1716; married Sarah Abbot; died Sept. 18, 1795.

6. Isaac Warren, 7th child of Elisha Warren; born July 30, 1758; died March 19, 1834; married Mary Swan, July 8, 1781, who died 1782.

   2d wife, Sept. 10, 1783, Elizabeth (Betsey) Warren, who was born Nov. 8, 1757, and died June 19, 1809. By her were two sons: —

   1. Dr. Isaac Warren, 3d; born Aug. 9, 1787; died Oct. 13, 1815.

   2. Amos Warren; born Aug. 29, 1789; died Aug. 14, 1814.

   3d wife, July 1, 1810, Abigail Fiske, widow of Isaac Lamson, of Weston, who was born April 4, 1769, and died May 19, 1858.

7. George Washington Warren, son of Isaac Warren and Abigail Fiske; born at Charlestown, Oct. 1, 1813; died May 13, 1883.

FISKE.

[*Bond, p. 214.*]

1. Nathan Fiske, settled in Waltham, 1642.

2. Nathan Fiske; born Oct. 17, 1642; died Oct., 1694.

3. (Deacon) Nathan Fiske; born Jan. 3, 1672–3; died 1741; married Sarah Coolidge, Oct. 14, 1696.

4. Nathan Fiske; born Feb. 25, 1701–2; married Oct. 9, 1730, Anne Warren, who died Oct. 1, 1736; married Feb. 1, 1738–9, Mary Fiske.

5. Jonathan Fiske; born Dec. 15, 1739; married April 30, 1760, Abigail Fiske.

6. Abigail Fiske, child of Jonathan Fiske and Abigail Fiske; born April 4, 1769; married 2d time, Isaac Warren, July 1, 1810; died May 19, 1858.

7. George Washington Warren, son of Isaac Warren and Abigail Fiske Warren.

LETTERS

CHARLESTOWN, March 4, 1822.

MY DEAR GEORGE, — I received yours of the 18th ult., and am much gratified to learn that you are in good health, and like your place and studies. You mention you should like to have me write to you. It will, I assure you, afford me much pleasure to write to you if I find you endeavor to make a good and useful improvement of my letters.

I feel great satisfaction in your being placed where I hope you daily receive good *moral instructions,* as well as in your studies; yet I should be greatly deficient in the love and affection of a tender parent if I did not feel a great concern for your good deportment, your improvement in learning, and a solicitude for your present and future happiness. You are now, my child, old enough to begin to form a kind of youthful character, in the seminary and family, which will be a foundation for a more permanent character if you live to grow up to manhood. I have often told you that you have everything to encourage and stimulate you to exert yourself to make the best improvement of the advantages you enjoy to obtain a good education, and thereby be qualified for usefulness in the world. And do not, my dear child, think that you are too young to be reminded of your duty to your heavenly Father, and that you were born for an endless eternity, and how very uncertain your life is, even in childhood. It is found that in this town about one-half the number that have died (in some years) have been under ten years of age; remember that your life is as uncertain as any other. How important is it, then, that you, even in your childhood, should strive to cultivate a supreme love to God, your Saviour and Redeemer, and a delight in reading and committing to memory the sacred scriptures!

I must again charge you to attend diligently to your studies — to conduct well in the school — to the preceptor, to Mr. Webster and the family.

I am sorry to hear that some of the children have been unwell; hope before this time they have regained their health.

Agreeable to your request I send you a Bible, though I cannot account for it how you have lost the other.

Give our regard to Mr. and Mrs. Webster, and to Mr. Vose, and remember the instructions of your

Affectionate parent,

I. WARREN.

N.B. — When you write again be sure to write all the inside with your own hand, that I may know how you improve in writing.

I charge you to keep the letters I send you, and when you come home bring them with you.

I keep all your letters for you to look on, if you live ten years hence, that you may see how much you improve.

In your next letter give me some account of the seminary, and think of some subject to make a longer letter.

If you can't read this you may let Mr. Webster read it.

P.S. — Since writing the above I have received your letter of the 8th inst. Your mam. has been so engaged in getting poor Mary's things ready that she has not had time to attend to your clothes; but we shall endeavor to send them to you without fail before the time you mention. Will send your other hat with them.

Mr. Bennett preached for Mr. Fay [1] last week. He and Mary remember you. Why don't you mention them in your letters?

I send you a Bible, and charge you to be careful of it.

---

[1] Rev. Dr. Fay, Pastor First Church in Charlestown.

CHARLESTOWN, June 21, 1822.

MY DEAR CHILD: — I embrace this favorable opportunity to send a line to you tho' I have but a few moments to write.

Your letter enclosing one to Joseph and Mary was received. They were very much gratified with it.

It is very pleasing to us to hear Mr. Webster speak so well of you, that you attend so well to your studies, and like the place so well. We cannot but hope that you will be a fine scholar, a *good man*, and a great *comfort to us*. I intend to write a longer letter when I have time.

Present our regards to Mr. and Mrs. Webster, Mr. Vose, and Miss Tewksbury.

Remember to improve your time well, and to be a good child, and to evidence your love and affection for your indulgent parents,

I. AND A. WARREN.

N.B. — You can send letters almost every week to Mr. Webster, at Boston.

————

CHARLESTOWN, July 10, 1822.

MY DEAR GEORGE: — It seems a long time since I have heard from you. I hope your health is continued, and that you are making the best improvement of your time in laying a foundation for such an education as may qualify you for a good, virtuous, and useful member of society. You have everything to encourage you that a child could wish for; be very careful, then, that nothing on your part shall be wanting to make you beloved and respected. I consider it of no less importance that you learn to cultivate a submissive, *good disposition* than the studies in your education, — a truly pious and virtuous mind with a good temper and disposition I consider of more value than the learning of all the philosophers that ever lived, even if they could (with Sir Isaac Newton) count the stars in the heavens!

Joseph and Mary are gone to an ordination. Mary intends staying with Mrs. Mann at Weston, while Mr. Bennett went on to the ordination.

Give our kind respects to Mr. and Mrs. Webster, and Mr. Vose, and Miss Tewksbury. Write the first opportunity to
Your affectionate parents,
I. AND A. WARREN.

N.B.—Your letter to Mr. B. and Mary was very pleasing to them. You must write to them again.

CHARLESTOWN, Sept. 22, 1822.

MY DEAR GEORGE: — I have received two letters from you this term. Have intended to write to you before, but have waited for an opportunity of private conveyance. I have been unwell the past week, but am now much better.

In your letter you have given me a short account of your school. I am glad to find that you like Mr. Cummings so well. Hope the Academy will not suffer by Mr. Vose's leaving. I hope Mr. Cummings feels the importance of giving moral and religious instructions to the youth under his care, as I consider it the most important part of their education. I should never be willing to place a child where this was not attended to. I believe that children are capable of being taught their duty to God, to love their Saviour and Redeemer, and, in some measure, to understand the principles of religion, at as early an age as any other branch of their education. I hope, my dear child (however raggish you are when at home), that you are now more sedate and steady, and that your conduct and deportment, both in the family and school, will be becoming the name of " young gentlemen," as you say there are five boarders with Mr. Webster, " of which you are one."

Mr. Fay has been preaching to-day on the vast importance of giving children an early *religious education.* I have long been impressed with the same idea, and have endeavored to act from the same principle. Do not, my child, think that you are too young to be put in mind of death, judgment, and eternity. A great portion of those that have died of late in this vicinity were younger than you. You must not forget that your life, as well as others, is altogether uncertain. Remember the very sudden death of that lovely child of Mr. Flint's. You are no less liable to be snatched away by a sudden death. Oh, then, think how important to be prepared for so solemn and awful a change!

I do not wish you to deny yourself proper time for play, — some is necessary for exercise, — but don't give your mind too much to it; but try to excel in your improvement in studies and a manly deportment, especially in the family and at table. If you possess a real filial and grateful mind, you will, by attending to my instructions, greatly add to the enjoyment of your affectionate parent,

I. WARREN.

Since writing the foregoing I had the pleasure of seeing Mr. Cummings, at Andover. He tells me you had got the books that you sent for. I have, therefore, omitted sending the one I had procured for you.

Your grandmother has been here seven weeks. She expects to go away this week.

We have nothing remarkably interesting in this place.

When you write to me again you must write a good, long letter. And see how well you can make the writing and spelling appear.

Agreeable to your request, I send your hat; but expect you will not use it only to wear to meeting.

I have written you a long letter. Hope you will read it twice at least, and remember to improve from the counsel and advice of your parent.

I. WARREN.

CHARLESTOWN, Nov. 8th, 1822.

DEAR SON: — From your repeated request, in your letters, that I would often write to you, I am encouraged to hope you will make some good and useful improvement of the instructions I endeavor to communicate to you in my letters. Notwithstanding my great solicitude for your improvement and good deportment, I do not expect you to be possessed of the maturity of manhood while you are but a child in years; but, if I can but make you sensible, and realize how much my happiness, as well as your own, depends on your good habits, your attention to your education, your filial love and affection to your parents, and, above all, a sense of your duty to God and early impressions of a sincere love to your Saviour and Redeemer, — if these things might have a proper effect on your youthful mind, how it would stimulate you to the utmost exertions to excel all of your age in improvement and manly deportment! It is not, however, my wish to have you deprived of your sports and childish play, — exercise and innocent amusement are necessary for your health, if kept within proper bounds. There is a kind of dignity that even children are capable of observing, in the midst of their recreations, by strictly guarding against every kind of rude, naughty, mean, and unbecoming conduct with their playmates and in the family they live. In the academy I hope you will be studious and attentive to instruction, with the character of a *good scholar.* As this term draws near the close, I want you to prepare your mind, with more firm resolutions than ever (if you come home), to make the vacation agreeable, and a pleasant visit with us, by your manly deportment, instead of running away your flesh by driving a hoop! I should rather pay your board, and not have you come home in the vacation, than to have you drive about with all the rude boys and acquire bad habits. It has been some doubt in my mind whether it is best to have you come home; but I shall be better able to judge of your improvement and what progress you make in your education. This, however, you must understand, and firmly agree to (if you come home) that you will not run about or play with rude and bad boys; that you will endeavor to make yourself pleasant and agreeable in the family, especially at the table, and that in all respects you will evidence a kind, filial, and good disposition.

Oh, could your youthful mind but once realize how much your compliance with these counsels would add to the happiness, comfort, and enjoyments of your parents, as well as add to your own, you surely would feel the importance of making every exertion in your power! I do not like the idea of hiring you to be a good child; but this I may say: you have everything you can wish for to stimulate and encourage you to excel in every youthful improvement; and, above all, in the early cultivation of your mind, and a really good disposition of heart. You may write me a good long letter the first opportunity, and tell me whether (if you come home) you will strive to comply with these counsels, that your company may add to our enjoyment.

In these long evenings I want you to attend some to reading, as well as your studies, in some interesting and useful history, as well as moral subjects, that you may from your reading furnish your youthful mind with proper subjects to write upon in your letters to me and others.

The acquisition of human knowledge is slow, but ought always to be progressive, even from our childhood. I do not, my dear child, write to you with the expectation that you will only run over this letter and then throw it by without reading it the second time. It is my most ardent hope and my earnest prayer that you may be led and guided by these instructions, and that you may, years hence, when your mind and views may be more enlarged, receive important advantage from my paternal advice to you. I can judge but little of your improvement in your studies; but I want, *very much*, to have you exert yourself to improve in your writing and spelling. These are noble acquisitions, and do not require so much maturity of age as some other branches of education.

With the most tender concern for your happiness,

I am your affectionate parent,

I. WARREN.

Master G. WARREN.

N.B. — Write to me soon, and tell me whether you want to come home. If you come home let the stage man bring you and your trunk to the house. I expect you to write me a long and handsome letter, that I may see whether you make any improvement in writing and spelling.

CHARLESTOWN, Jan. 1, 1823.

MY DEAR GEORGE: — Your letter of the 20th ultimo was duly received. I am glad to find you had a pleasant ride down, and that you have again commenced your studies. As the winter is considered the most favorable time for study I expect you will make great proficiency in your learning this term. With a little more close attention to your spelling, and the form and shape of your letters, you might soon improve very much in your writing. You should always have a dictionary by you, when you write letters, and always look for words that you are not sure of spelling right. In your reading I want you to acquire a habit of reading louder and with more emphasis.

I have often expressed this to you : that you have everything you can wish for to encourage and stimulate you to exert yourself to the utmost, to make the best improvement in your power to acquire a good and useful education ; and be assured you can't begin too young to make yourself respectable and beloved, both in the family and academy. There is a kind of respect and dignity that even children may acquire, by evidencing a *good disposition* and a *cheerful, willing* subjection, and proper respect to those whom it is their duty to obey. If I find, my dear George, that you attend to my advice, and endeavor to make my letters useful to you, it will encourage me to write the oftener.

It is unaccountable what became of your penknife. If I am not very much mistaken I put it, myself, into the little box in your trunk. It is rather curious how you lose so many knives. I find no difficulty in keeping the same penknife upwards of forty years.

I think it would be an excellent good thing for you to go into some good farmer's family this summer and learn something of what it is to work, or you will never know how to manage a garden like your brother Joseph; besides, it would be an excellent thing to form and establish a good firm constitution.

If you can't find enough in your pericranium you must have recourse to some of your books for materials or subjects to write upon.

Your affectionate parent,

I. WARREN.

N.B. — If you write to me again you must be sure to make your letters richly worth the postage.

CHARLESTOWN, March 23, 1823.

MY DEAR GEORGE: — It is now a number of weeks since I wrote to you. I should not have delayed writing so long, but have been daily expecting a return from you.

I was exceedingly gratified by the account Mr. Cummings gave me in his letter, of the serious impressions of some of the students in the academy, and of some others in the place; and what has greatly added to my joy is to find that you have, at times, been deeply affected. Be assured, my dear child, it has been, with me, a subject of unceasing prayer to God, that you may, even in your childhood and youth, be led to embrace the Saviour and Redeemer, who so freely offers to receive, and graciously to pardon and accept of, even *children*, that sincerely come unto him in the way pointed out in the sacred scriptures. You have heard and read enough in the Bible to learn something of the precious invitations and promises there made, — that "those that seek me early shall find." I hope, my dear child, that you will unite with me in my daily prayers for you, that these impressions may not be transient, and soon wear off;

but, O, blessed Saviour, may they be deep and lasting, and may you be led by the blessed Spirit to a knowledge of your duty, and as you have been given up to God by baptism, in your infancy, and are under covenant obligations to him, — oh, that you may early be interested in the blessings of that covenant of grace! This is infinitely more valuable than all the possessions and learning in the world. I should have many things more to say to you, to encourage and stimulate you to exert yourself to the utmost of your abilities in your studies in every branch of your education, — and more especially in the cultivation of your mind, and forming a system of religious and virtuous habits,— but the term being so near out, and you probably will be with us in about a fortnight, I shall omit writing on these subjects, in hopes when you come home I shall have an opportunity for much improvement in useful and interesting conversation. I hope, therefore, you will come home with a fixed resolution not only to begin, but to persevere in the most useful, pleasant, and agreeable manner of spending your time, a part of which shall be devoted to visiting our friends.

26th March. — This day Mr. Green is to be installed at Essex-street Church, in Boston. Mr. Bennett is on the Council. He and Mary came here yesterday. Mary sends her love to you.

I shall not make up my mind fully where to have you go the coming season, until you come home; I would, therefore, have you to be sure to bring all your things home, together with your books and writings. It will be no great inconvenience to bring them if you should return to Hampton.

Give my affectionate regards to Mr. and Mrs. Webster, and remember all the good instructions you receive from them, and from your indulgent parent,

I. WARREN.

———

CHARLESTOWN, April 15, 1823.

DEAR SON: — Having had some thoughts of coming down after you I have omitted writing till this evening. But as the weather is so uncertain, and I have not been very well of late,

I have concluded to have you come home in the stage. You will remember what I wrote to you in my last letter, to bring home all your things, as I cannot fully determine where I shall have you go the next term until you come home. I should be much gratified to be present at your examination, but it is not convenient for me to be so long from home. I hope we shall find your improvements in the cultivation of your mind, as well as your learning, to be such as shall give me a still higher estimation of the academy.

As I expect to see you so soon you must be content with a short letter. Present our affectionate regards to Mr. and Mrs. Webster, Mr. Cummings, and Miss T.

I anticipate your visit with much pleasure, and hope you will not disappoint the hopes of your fond parent,

I. WARREN.

N.B. — You will request Mr. Webster to send his bill, and, if he has time, to write me a letter.

The enclosed bill I send to you.

CHARLESTOWN, May 28, 1823.

DEAR GEORGE: — I received your short letter by Major Lovering. I am sorry to find you had no better subject to write upon than that of cutting your handkerchiefs to pieces. It was a crime that ought, in some way, to be punished; but as you acknowledge your fault, and appear to be sorry for it, I shall pass it over and forgive you this time, on the condition that you will, in future be careful of your things, and not lose nor needlessly waste your things, and that in all your deportment you strive to be discreet and prudent, and conduct yourself so as to gain the love and esteem of your friends, and your indulgent parents,

I. AND A. WARREN.

P.S. — Major Lovering will probably be up again in June. You must write by him. I hope you will write something more interesting. Your mam. will have your summer clothes to send by him.

Our friends like to see your letters; you must not send any that you would be ashamed to have seen.

I write this in great haste. Shall write to you again when I have time.

CHARLESTOWN, July 24, 1823.

MY DEAR GEORGE: — I have this instant received your letter of the 22d. It gives me pleasure to hear from you, and to find that your letters are more interesting than they were months past. I hope you are making good improvements in every branch of your education.

You speak of my not writing often, and of my forgetting you. I can assure you that you are not out of my mind many waking hours of my life. I want you to be sensible how much I think of you, and how solicitous I feel for your improvement, especially for the cultivation of your mind, and good moral virtuous habits, that you may be qualified for, and made useful and respectable in the world, and a great comfort to your parents and friends; and, above all, if you live to manhood, that you may be instrumental of doing much good in promoting the cause and interest of vital religion, and thereby glorifying God, your Saviour and Redeemer.

I charge you, my dear child, not to forget these things, and, when the hand that is now writing to you is mouldering in the dust, that you (if you live) often read over my letters, and let the counsels and instructions which I have given you have a deep impression on your youthful mind; and oh, may the blessings of your heavenly Father ever rest upon you, and guard you against the snares and temptations of this sinful world, and lead and guide you in the path to virtue and permanent happiness! Your brother and sister Bennett were here yesterday. They are well. I shall show them your letter, as you mention them in so friendly manner in yours. You must not send any letters that you should be ashamed your friends should read. It is therefore important for you, and even for your academy, that you should take particular care that your letters should be handsomely written, and superscribed; for, if they should never be printed, they may probably be kept for half a century.

You mention about my coming to examination; but it is not likely that I shall. I may write to you again before that time.

I have nothing particularly interesting to tell you, only that there have been about forty-five joined the church here since you left us.

I went to Weston last week, carried your uncle Nathan's Mary home, who had passed two or three weeks with us. She is going to Mr. Emerson's school again next term. Friends are well at Weston.

You have improved in your writing; but still I want to have you make your letters more plain, round and fair, which is very easy by care and attention, if you have a good pen, which is very necessary to write well, and which it can't be expected you can make yourself. I want you to give me some evidence in your letters of your love of books, by your studies and reading, geography, histories, etc. You may introduce some interesting selections from your reading.

You mention that you expect Mr. Cummings will leave after the close of this term. I hope whoever comes will maintain and support proper discipline and good government in the school, without which the young gentlemen had much better be at work on a farm.

I can't tell you now where I shall think best to place you the next term. I can judge better when I find what improvement you have made.

Sam'l Fay has gone to Andover Academy. He is admitted into our church. Mr. Fay is contemplating a journey to the springs, to be absent three or four weeks. How should you like to go with him?

Isaac Henry's grandpa was here some time ago. They are not coming down to make us a visit till the fall, when I should like to have you see each other. The time is fast approaching when he must be placed in some academy. I shall then have two to write to.

Accept of love from your mother and other friends.

Give my kind regards to all inquiring friends.

Having filled my sheet, I have only room to say to you that, if you mean to be a truly *great man*, you must be virtuous and good while young, and always remember the advice of your affectionate parent,

I. WARREN.

N.B. — If I don't write again before you come home, I would have you bring home all your things.

And don't come home again without your bill.

———

CHARLESTOWN, October 6, 1823.

DEAR GEORGE: — Your letter, dated more than a week since, came to hand this morning. I have been very anxious to hear from you. It is very gratifying to find you are so well pleased with your situation. I hope you will not fail of making the best improvement from the great advantages you are so highly favored with. I wish it was possible for me deeply to impress on your mind the importance of beginning in early life to form a respectable, manly character, that your conduct and deportment, even in your youth, may in all respects be such as to lay a good foundation for a virtuous, dignified manhood, which, if you live, may entitle you to that respectable station in society to which your parents and friends have a just right to hope and expect you will acquire.

I have often told you, and again put you in mind of it, that I consider it an important part of your education that you endeavor to cultivate your mind with a *good disposition*; by this I mean those amiable qualities and virtuous habits which may render your future life pleasant, useful, and happy. I had much rather see you possess these virtues than all the riches this world can give, and learning enough to count the stars, without those qualities of heart calculated to make you both useful and happy. As to your studies, I shall submit to the judgment of your preceptor. It is, however, my wish that you attend to *reading*, *writing*, and *spelling*. I think these are the branches most easily attained at your age, and the most important to qualify you for usefulness. Other branches of studies are good in their place.

It makes but a miserable appearance to figure away in Latin with but poor writing and bad spelling. If you intend to be a good scholar, you must pay more attention to these branches. I want to see you write a good, fair hand, plain and easy to read. Nothing is more easy to learn (except it is to play) than it is to write a good hand. It only requires care and attention both to write and spell correctly.

I hope you will not forget what I have so often enjoined upon you, that your conduct and deportment in the family should always be with all proper subjection and respectful attention, *especially at the table*. These qualities, accompanied with a *good disposition*, form a correct criterion to judge of the future character of the man.

In addition to the good example and instructions you will receive in all the moral virtues, I trust you will frequently be put in mind of the importance of religion, and that your youthful mind will *early* be led to the study and love of the sacred scriptures, and to feel the obligations you are under to love and devote yourself to the Divine Saviour and Redeemer. As to your deportment in school hours, I have nothing to say, having the fullest confidence in your preceptor.

I have nothing very interesting to acquaint you with. Your Mam. has been at Woburn about ten days, and I have been almost alone.

Your brother Bennett and Mary are well. They have spent two nights with us this week. I believe they do not contemplate coming to Framingham this autumn.

Give our kind regards to Mr. and Mrs. Warren and all the family. We don't give up the idea of visiting them this fall, but it is altogether uncertain.

I intended writing to Mr. Pike, but have not time at present. You will present my respects to him and Mrs. P., and tell them we should be glad to see them at our house.

You must send us a good, long letter, and let us see what improvement you make in your writing. I must enjoin it upon you to be more attentive, and make your letters more correct, round, and handsome, and endeavor to improve in every acquisition that may qualify you for (what I believe you mean to be) a useful and good man.

From your affectionate parent,

I. WARREN.

CHARLESTOWN, Dec. 12, 1823.

DEAR GEORGE: — I have so lately written to you that I seem to have nothing new to say to you, and yet the affectionate and tender feelings that entwine around and flow from the parental heart ought never to be satisfied with past exertions, but should improve every opportunity to give good advice and useful instructions to their children. You have often expressed a wish that I would frequently write to you. Now, the only way to induce me to write is, for you to pay a strict attention to the counsels and advice which I give you. However young and volatile you now feel, I want you to remember that *precious time*, even in childhood and youth, is valuable, and ought to be improved to some good purpose. I don't wish you to be debarred from proper exercise and play, but I entreat you to keep it in mind that now is the time for you, by diligent attention to the various branches of education, to lay a good foundation for a respectable character and a useful member of society. If you live to manhood, and make this happy choice, it will in no small degree add to the enjoyment of your connections, and especially to your affectionate parents,

I. AND A. WARREN.

N.B. — Remember, kind love to all your Uncle Warren's family.

MY DEAR SON: — In the few lines I wrote to you by Major Wheeler I promised you a longer letter soon. Your two last letters afford me some encouraging hope that you are making good improvement in your education.

You have often expressed what you mean to be when you become a man; but whether your youthful ambition will prompt you to shine in the Elysian fields of science and literature, and in all their arduous heights and profound depths, or whether your inclination (as you seem lately to think it may) will incline you to a more busy scene and active employment in the bustle of trade and merchandise, is yet altogether uncertain. One thing, however, is certain, if you mean to be useful, respectable, and happy in the world, you must, even in your childhood, exert *your own energies;* for, be assured of this, that all the advantages you enjoy, and all that is expended for your education, will, in a great measure, be lost without your own close and industrious application in a manner that shall evidence that you are in earnest to make the best improvements in your power. If you ask me how you should commence this course, I would answer, in the first place, by all means let your moral conduct be pure and free from every stain; let there be the most rigid and sacred regard to *truth* in all your conversation and dealings with others, however small, yet no less important to be strictly correct. Let your deportment in the family and school always be modest, unassuming, and pleasant, and to your schoolmates affable and engaging. And if you wish for an enlarged and comprehensive view of the various branches of the philosophy of the human mind, and the intellectual improvement of your youthful capacities, you must by degrees acquire a habit of and a relish for reading; for no one can expect to be intelligent, happy, and useful to himself and his fellow-creatures without the culture and discipline of a well-regulated mind, especially that most of all important science, a *virtuous and good disposition.* This, in my view, is infinitely more valuable than all the learning in the world without it. To acquire this, a love of books, and a habit of reading with some degree of system, are very useful and important. And you may rest assured of this, that the more you give yourself to reading, and the more knowledge you acquire, the greater thirst you will have for improvement.

It is important, when your mind is more matured, that you acquire a refined and correct taste in your choice of books, for in reading a bad selection of authors the time is far worse than lost.

There is, my dear child, one subject more I ought not to pass unnoticed, which is still more important. I mean the great concern which we were sent into the world for; namely, to prepare for an endless state of existence beyond the grave. I hope you have not wholly lost the impressions you formerly appeared to have on this subject. It is certainly of the first importance that the minds of children, even in their early youth, should be directed to this interesting subject; and I should not discharge the duty of a parent to a child whom I feel a great concern and solicitude for, if I neglected to give you some counsel and advice on a subject so important for your present enjoyment as well as future happiness. Having, however, nearly filled my sheet, I must defer this for the subject of another letter.

The time occupied in writing to you, I hope, will not be lost. I must judge more favorably than to think you will run over my letters but once, and throw them by never to read them again. This would but poorly compensate me for writing. If some parts of my letters are calculated for one of more riper years than you are at present, my anxious solicitude for you induces me to hope that, in some future day, when the hand that wrote them may be mouldering in the dust, you will read the letters I now address to you with a more feeling concern, and a heart more deeply impressed with their importance, and as coming from the hand and attended with the prayers of your affectionate parent,

I. WARREN.

CHARLESTOWN, Nov. 5, 1824.

DEAR GEORGE: — Yours of the 25th ult., was duly received. I am much gratified with the filial affection and gratitude you

express for me, and your endeavors to improve my parental
counsel and advice to you. I am glad you are so well pleased
with your instructor, and your boarding-place. Your situation
being so highly favorable, in every respect, I hope your improvement will be commensurate with your peculiar advantages,
and that the farther you progress in your studies the more you
will find your mind engaged with a love and fondness for books.
I would, however, by no means wish you to be debarred from
devoting a proper portion of your time to unbend the mind, by
exercise and even playful diversion; this is necessary to keep
up the vigor of mind as well as bodily health. But I want
you to keep in mind that even your playful diversions should
be such as would not be unbecoming the laudable ambition of
a very young member of college.

It is not, by any means, my wish that your mind should be
burdened with things above your youthful capacity; but you
may be assured of this, that no age is too young to be impressed with a sense of the value and worth of precious time,
and the importance of imbibing habits of industry, even in
childhood and youth.

You are, my dear child, old enough to have some ideas of
what you were brought into existence for, and that this world
is but a short state of trial and probation to prepare for an
eternal state beyond the grave.

As you grow in years, and your youthful mind opens and
expands by cultivation and improvement, with the flattering
hopes of enjoyment and usefulness in the world, how proper it
is, even in early youth, to extend your views with the deepest
solicitude to those things which, on a moment's reflection, you
must be sensible involve your most durable and important
interest and happiness, both in the present and future world.
If, as you grow in years, you give me evidence that you possess
a disposition that shall incline you willingly and cheerfully to
attend to the good instructions and advice you receive from me,
I can assure you, it will be (under the loss of former children)
one of the greatest sources of enjoyment of anything this
world can afford me.

You don't say a word in your letters about college, or

whether you expect to be fitted to enter the next year. I am the more desirous to have you go as soon as you can, since your cousin, N. W. Fiske, has been made a professor there; it being uncertain how long he will continue, I should like to have you get through college while he is there.

I have lately been reading Cowper's private letters that were never published before; they are very interesting; I should like very well to have you read them. They were written at the time he was so closely engaged in translating Homer. It is astonishing to see how he persevered with such unwearied application for six years in that laborious work.

This was accomplished about forty years ago; possibly, by the time you graduate, another translation may be called for, — whether you will engage in it, or not, I will not undertake to prognosticate. I can only say, if you should, I hope you will succeed as well as he did.

There is an art and facility of expression and easy flow of language in letter-writing which, tho' I never could attain to it, I wish very much that you, with all your advantages of education may, in due time acquire. It is a talent, however desirable, very few in reality possess, of writing with about the same ease and without much more study than in common conversation; and yet their letters read very well. To acquire this talent I think the frequent reading of such authors as Newton and Cowper, and some others that were eminent for letter-writing, is very useful, especially for young people. Though I would not encourage downright plagiarism, yet by an attention to such authors and making ourselves familiar with their easy flow of language, we imbibe their ideas, and, in some measure, transform them into our minds and make them our own.

If what I have written to you may be better calculated for one of more riper years, I hope, when that time arrives, if you live, it will not be useless to you. I should think my time in writing to you was but poorly repaid if you only read my letters over once and put them out of sight, without any further attention to them; this I trust will not be the case, for I can assure you that I entertain very strong and flattering hopes of your being, not only a forward, good scholar, but, what is more important, a virtuous, amiable youth, — a great, useful, and good man.

That a kind Providence may vouchsafe to bless and succeed my exertions to be, in some measure, instrumental in promoting this, is, I hope, the sincere and ardent prayer of your affectionate parent,

ISAAC WARREN.

P.S. — You mention about coming home in the stage.

I have thought of coming after you, if the weather and travelling is good.

I shall want to know when the examination is. Probably Mr. J. Warren will be down before the time. If he should, I wish you would ask him to come over to Charlestown.

———

CHARLESTOWN, March 30, 1825.

DEAR SON: — Yours, of the 28th inst., was received this morning. I am sorry to find that you appear so unwilling to exert yourself to be fitted to enter college the next commencement. You speak about being ashamed to have it told that you were going next commencement, and have Mr. Cheney say you were not fitted. I told you before that I should not expect, or wish, you to be offered the next fall, unless he approved of it, and thought you might be admitted without "squeezing" in. You know Mr. Cheney expressed his opinion, the last term, that you might, with good attention, be prepared for Amherst the next fall, and that it was rather unfavorable for students to be too forward when they enter, and rather endanger their good habits of industry and close application to studies. Altho' I had fixed my mind on your going to college the next season I am not so anxious about that as I am to have your moral conduct and deportment correct and free from every stain, especially from every kind of deception, prevarication, or falsehood. I conjure you in the most solemn manner, with all the tender and parental feelings of an affectionate father, that you do not trifle with my advice to you in this respect. I wish it was possible for me to convince you that you are now laying a foundation for a character that will follow you (if you live) to manhood, and how exceedingly important it is for you, as well as your friends and connections, that even in your childhood and youth you should practise none other but *correct and virtuous habits.* Any deviation from this moral rectitude of deportment, especially anything like deception or falsehood, will fix a stain on the youthful character that will not easily be erased.

I am willing you should indulge a laudable ambition, and look forward to the time when, if you exert yourself to cultivate your mind and make the best improvement in your power, you may rise to some eminence and respectability in the world ; and, therefore, I charge you to guard against everything that has the appearance of being mean and contemptible, — that all your conduct, your conversation and deportment may be *open and frank.* This, instead of a downcast look, will give a countenance that will appear with a cheerful smile of innocence. And now I again charge you, my child, if you wish to secure and increase my affectionate parental love and esteem for you, that you *resolve* to act on the principle I have laid down for you to govern yourself from, and endeavor to give evidence that you are constantly aiming to possess that elevation and nobleness of mind that is calculated to add a kind of dignity to the character even of a youth. Be sure to let this maxim govern you through the whole course of your education ; and, if you are ever unfortunate, by losing anything, or are in particular want of money, or anything else, never, never make use of any deceptive arts to obtain your object, or to cover and hide a fault. This would not only tend to make your own mind unhappy, but would tend greatly to discourage and dishearten parents in complying with your wishes. After all that I can say to you, I shall despair of its having the happy effect which I so ardently wish for, unless your mind is brought to feel a deep sense of the moral obligation you are under to love and respect the institutions of religion, and to devote yourself in your early youth to your Saviour and Redeemer. For this, my dear child, I desire daily to breathe out a devout prayer to Him who has promised " that those that seek me early shall find me."

In your letters to me you should always take some notice of the contents of the last letter received from me, with some remarks and observations on the subjects alluded to, that it may be evident that you have paid due attention to the instructions and advice which I endeavor, with the tender concern of an affectionate parent, to communicate to you.

Julia's sister, Maria D., is now with us, and Uncle Nathan. Mary has been with us the past week. Maria is going to Camden to keep a school there this summer. She brought me a pretty letter from your nephew, Isaac Henry. He desires to be remembered to you, and hopes to come to the academy in the course of the year. Present my kind regards to Mr. Cheney and all the family, and be sure to write a good, handsome letter *soon* to your parent,

ISAAC WARREN.

BOSTON, April 28, 1825.

DEAR SON : — I am much disappointed to find that the things I left at the office yesterday for Mr. Warren to carry to you, were not gone. I presume he called for them while they were gone to dinner.

I am now waiting at the office to see some gentleman, and therefore improve the time in writing a few lines more to you.

Having an invitation, I went, on Tuesday, to the exhibition at Cambridge College. I wish you could have been there; some of the performances were very good, and some I thought you could have done about as well. A Greek dialogue on marriage was the most amusing; but the last oration on *education* was by far the most interesting. It was delivered by the son of our secretary, Major Cunningham. I should admire to have you get it to speak at your next examination. I am very fond of hearing public speaking, when both the subject and manner of delivery are interesting. There are, however, but few that possess the qualification of real, *graceful eloquence.* This is what I am exceedingly desirous you should fix your aim at, and that to a good degree of eminence. I believe you want nothing but industry, and a good degree of laudable ambition, fully to acquire it.

Under the fostering care and guidance of your kind heavenly Father, with a proper reliance on the grace and strength of your divine Saviour and Redeemer, and the great advantages you enjoy for acquiring a good education, you have only to resolve and persevere in it, that you will by your industry, together with a noble, dignified, manly, yet modest, deportment, make yourself, not only respectable, but somewhat eminent. But you must remember that no one can be called *truly* a great man that is not a *good* man, or one that possesses real virtue and religion. That you may live to be useful and do much good in the world and be prepared for a happier state beyond the grave is the daily prayer of your parent,

I. W.

N.B. — I have waited an opportunity to send your things and this letter; shall now send by Mr. Levi Warren.

It is not certain about my coming up at the examination, but think it probable I shall, if it is pleasant weather. I want you to ask Mr. Cheney to let you have a part in Greek. My greatest request is that you may be strictly ingenuous, manly, and dignified in your deportment, with your endeavors to be qualified to do great good in the world.

I shall inquire particularly of Mr. Cheney respecting your books, and shall procure whatever he shall think proper, — that nothing may be wanting for your improvement; only exert yourself to compensate me by a grateful reception of all that is done for you.

CHARLESTOWN, May 10, 1825.

DEAR SON: — Yours of the 7th inst. is received. I have noted its contents. Before this comes to your hand you will have received my letter and some of the things that you have been so solicitous about. As to the books, which you have so often mentioned, I thought the term was so near out that it was not important to procure them until I should see you and know what is wanting.

The other things which you mention with so much solicitude, such as handkerchief, pin, penknife, etc., etc., — I am sorry to find that such trifling things occupy so much of your attention. I would fain have you ambitious for the acquisition of more noble and important objects, — that your letters may be filled with something more deeply interesting. Children that have the advantages which you have never ought to write a letter to their parents that they would need to be ashamed to have printed! I hope, however, as you grow older, your letters will have more of the complexion of a mind not only well cultivated, but, as it were, soaring after more elevated views and objects of a dignified and virtuous character, becoming the scholar and the truly wise and good man.

If nothing prevent I intend coming after you; it is uncertain whether I come on Thursday evening. I presume the examination will be most interesting in the afternoon. I shall probably leave your mam. at Weston, as we could not all ride comfortably. I have only room to add my sincere and ardent prayers that the blessings of a kind Providence may ever rest on you, and that you strive to promote the happiness of your indulgent parent,

I. WARREN.

N.B. — After receiving your letter mentioning about the black handkerchief you wanted, having a prospect of sending it, I went to Boston on purpose to get one for you. I hope you will be as willing to do for me.

CHARLESTOWN, Nov. 4, 1825.

DEAR GEORGE: — I have noticed the contents of your letter by Mr. Adams. Some of the sentiments contained in it give me encouraging hopes of your making rapid improvements under the peculiar advantages which it has fallen to your lot to be favored with. I trust we may entertain high hopes of you as a scholar. This, to be sure, might be gratifying to our worldly ambition, and is good so far as it proceeds from pure and correct motives; but I must entreat you to remember, and never — no, never — forget it, that all the Greek and Latin, and even all the literature and philosophy in the world, will never constitute a real eminent, great, and good man, without a strict attention to the moral character and amiable deportment which, with virtuous habits, is engaging in all classes of society, but more peculiarly so to the youthful student. What can afford more pleasure to the philanthropist and the pious, good man than to see a large class of students assiduously engaged in acquiring a useful education in all the different branches of literature, and at the same time making the utmost exertions in the more important science of cultivating their minds, and thereby laying a foundation for future eminence and usefulness in the world? And even this is not all I want to see you feel the importance of. I long to see you deeply impressed with a sense of your obligations to devote yourself in your early youth to your Creator, your Saviour and Redeemer. This, however you may consider it as of little importance, is, and shall ever, while I live, be my sincere and earnest prayer to God for you, with a humble hope that, however you may view these things at present, I may yet live to see the time when you will be convinced that real, vital religion is the only sure foundation for permanent happiness.

When you write again, which I hope will be soon, I shall expect the " good, long letter" promised some time since. You have, I presume, considerable time besides your regular hours of study, some of which I hope you will improve in cheerful, improving, and useful conversation, such as may be calculated to enlarge the mental powers and faculties of the mind. And I cannot but hope that some portion of your time every day, and especially every evening before you retire to your bed, be given to serious devotional exercises.

As I understand one of your chums is a professor of religion.

I hope he makes a practice of religious performances in your little family. If that has or should be practised I must entreat of you and charge you never to show any disapprobation or dislike to such performances, but endeavor to encourage and unite with them.

You would find it greatly to your improvement if you should acquire a correct taste for reading and writing letters. This is an important method of cultivating and improving in useful knowledge.

When you write to me again let it be like social conversation, giving me a more particular account of the college, of its most prominent features, and a general description of its government and regulations. And when you have a private conveyance again, send me one of your elegant catalogues. You may always send to the Union Bank, directed to Mr. Adams.

I wish you to give my regard to your room-mates, and tell them I should like to have them write to me. I intend writing to them when I find leisure.

Don't fail to keep my letters, and read them more than once.

In your letter you mention something about a college uniform; but I have no idea that it is expected the students are to throw away their present clothing for the sake of a uniform. This, however, is a subject that shall be attended to in due season. This you may rest assured of, that, if you will exert yourself to be a correct and good scholar, I shall not let you be behind others in your class as to whatever is necessary to give you a respectable standing in college.

We cannot think it necessary or expedient to get any new clothes till you come home; it will be much more convenient to get them here. And only think how soon the time will pass away! only about seven weeks to vacation. How do you think you shall pass away your long six weeks' vacation?

Our little family circle still enjoy the blessing of health, though there has been an unusual number of deaths among us of late. Four or five lay dead in town yesterday, among others, Mr. David Forsdick's wife and Mrs. Knowles.

We went to meeting at Woburn last Sabbath. Mr. Bennett

and Mary were well. They intend to come and see you next summer.

The book you mentioned that you should like to have, not being a classical book, I thought it could not be important for you at present, therefore did not like to trouble anybody to bring it, though I would if it was necessary.

Our little family send their love to you, — your nephew, Isaac H., among the rest. I hope you have not forgotten the subject of my former letter. Don't neglect to write soon to your affectionate parent,

ISAAC WARREN.

CHARLESTOWN, Nov. 16, 1825.

DEAR GEORGE: — I have for some time been waiting for the promised " good, long letter," until this evening I have, instead of a letter, received an enclosed catalogue ; this I thank you for, because you have complied with my request ; but if it had been accompanied with a " good, long letter," it would have been very gratifying to me. And, surely, with all your advantages of reading and studies, you can't be wanting for a subject to write upon. Those letters are most interesting that appear like *written conversation;* the style and manner of conversation, therefore, should be evident in epistolary writings. I wish you could surmount this aversion to letter-writing, and endeavor to cultivate your mind by industry and improvement, a correct taste and easy, familiar style of language ; you would find an important acquisition in your future attempts in composition.

The student, if he wish to enlarge his mind, inform his judgment, and improve his understanding, must not expect to live in ease and indolence. He must read, think, and digest, if he has any ambition to make himself eminent. Though I would recommend an industrious application to studies, yet, I would by all means have you guard against unnecessary *night studies,* which has ever been considered by physicians as very prejudicial to health. Dr. W——, in his letters, is very particular on this subject, of night studies, and states how very injurious it has often proved to the student, and that it ought to be avoided, that is to excess, by all who wish to prolong their lives, and make themselves useful in society.

There are many things I want to say to you, if I could only be assured that you would kindly receive, and endeavor to improve the advice and counsel which I assure you comes from the heart of an affectionate parent.

You will, no doubt, recollect that I have heretofore observed to you that the commencement of your college-life must, in every view, be considered a very important period of your life. It is hardly possible that a scholar of your age can realize the advantages or disadvantages of the habits which you form at this particular crisis. It is, therefore, of the first importance that you choose for your most intimate associates young men of steady and virtuous habits, those who are *resolutely* determined to be good and industrious students, and evidence a laudable ambition to be eminent, not only as good scholars, but also, what is of no small importance even in a youth, to appear to advantage by endeavoring to acquire a *modest, unassuming* deportment, and genteel address. These things may appear of little consequence to you now; but I can assure you that age, experience, and a knowledge of mankind, and human nature will convince you that they are of no small importance in laying the foundation and forming the character of an eminent man, as well as the scholar. I must, therefore, entreat of you, with all the affection of a tender parent, that you will read, more than once, and reflect on these things, and oh, let not my endeavors to advise, counsel, and instruct you be lost upon you! I once more charge you never to think, or say, that you need no advice, or that it will do no good. This you must and will be convinced of, that if good counsel and advice is not kindly received, it will, at a future day, prove a source of aggravation to you, that you ever enjoyed such high and exalted privileges for improvement both in literature and the means of religious instructions.

From your good improvement in your studies I can assure you that I anticipate with pleasure your still greater and more rapid progress.

There has been nothing particularly interesting taken place

here since you left us. Isaac Henry has been here and has gone to school, and learnt considerable. His mother has been with us about a fortnight.

After hearing from you, which I hope to soon, with giving me a particular account of your college concerns, I shall, probably, write to you again before the close of the term and your return home, when I hope we shall realize much pleasure in the evidence you will give us of your increasing improvement in every respect.

A gentleman, from Middlebury, Vt., tells me there has lately been serious attention paid to religion for weeks passed in the college in that place, and that many of the scholars have become subjects of religious impressions. It would be gratifying to the friends of Amherst College, to learn that a general attention to the subject of religion should ever be associated with their collegiate studies, and that the students generally might imbibe evangelical sentiments, and be led to turn their attention to theology and divinity. However you may at present feel an aversion to the idea of these studies, I cannot but entertain a hope that the time will come when your heart and your views will be changed, and that you may feel the importance of real, vital religion. I cannot, my dear child, close my letter without pressing this subject upon you with the most earnest solicitation, and entreat you to read, with attention, the precious promises made to those that *early* seek the Lord in their youthful days. That you may be preserved from every unfavorable habit and be led to embrace the precious promises in the gospel, is the ardent prayer of your affectionate parent,

I. WARREN.

P.S. — I have a strong and confident hope that the solemn advice which you found enclosed in my former letter will *never be forgotten.*

As to your uniform, clothing, etc., which you mention in your letter, I assure you that every reasonable request shall be attended to when you come home.

MY DEAR GEORGE: — It would only be repeating the old story if I were to begin my letter by saying that I have been anxiously waiting in expectation of your complying with my request of more frequently writing to me. I don't wish you to do this at any sacrifice of your studies, neither can I think this would be necessary, but I do think that a portion of your time devoted to the cultivation of the faculties, and mental powers of your mind, in writing letters and other compositions, would prove an important and very useful method of improving some of your leisure hours. Another important manner of improving time, even in your cheerful and playful relaxations, for necessary exercise, that you associate *only* with such as are respectable, manly in their deportment, interesting in their conversation, and of steady, good habits.

There is one remark in this connection which it would be well for every scholar to fix in his mind, viz.: that the conduct of students in college is much more known to the world than they can conceive of; there is scarcely anything more public than the good, or ill deportment of scholars in college. The eyes of their country are upon them, and the public have a kind of property and interest in their being qualified for, and making themselves *useful* and *eminent* in their day, by their exertions to improve their *special advantages* to promote both the temporal and spiritual happiness of their fellow-men.

If the community feel such a deep interest in the regular order and good deportment of students in college, with what anxious solicitude does the tender parent view the expanding mind, and anticipate the well-bred scholar and future eminence and piety of his only child.

I could fill whole sheets with this subject, but must leave it for the present, and earnestly entreat of you to let these few lines be felt with a deep and lasting impression on your heart.

As an encouragement to stimulate you in those noble exertions to excel as a student, I must tell you that I have had very favorable accounts of your good scholarship and progress in Greek.

As your term is so near the close, probably I shall not write to you again before you come home. Hope your vacation will prove, more than usual, interesting and happy to us and to you.

Your mam. wishes me to ask you to be *very particular* that you bring home all your clothes. You will do well to comply with her request, that she may see you have not left or lost anything.

I shall expect you to come in the same stage with Adams and Fay.

With my regards to the young gentlemen, your chums, I have only room for the name of your affectionate parent,

I. WARREN.

CHARLESTOWN, Jan. 23, 1827.

DEAR GEORGE: — It seems a long time since I have heard from you. I feel anxious to know how you are improving your time, and what progress you are making in your studies. I should think it could not be an unpleasant task to you to write more frequently to us, if it was only to express your sense of gratitude and filial respect of your parents. But this is not all, nor the greatest object; you would, by accustoming yourself to a habit of more frequently writing letters, and selecting and transcribing interesting and useful ideas from authors, acquire an easy flow of language, and facility of expression and composition, which is very important, even in a common education, and which can never be obtained in any other way but by practice. To one who has the advantage of education, and a happy talent of composition, writing must be an amusement rather than a task. I must enjoin it upon you that in future you will not let sloth and indolence, or anything else, prevent your resolutely persevering in a practice so useful for your improvement in common life as well as a scholar.

That we were formed for social intercourse in society is an unquestionable maxim; those acquirements, therefore, which will render us most amiable and useful to our fellow-creatures,

are objects worthy of our constant pursuit. Reading is un-
doubtedly one of the most important means of acquiring useful
knowledge; but the selection of authors and subjects should be
made with peculiar care and good judgment, and with a view to
promote the best effect and the most virtuous impressions on
the mind, — such as is calculated to enlighten the understanding, to enoble the mind, to give us high and exalted ideas
of the Supreme Being, and impress on our hearts an exalted
sense of the sacred scriptures. True wisdom allows nothing to
be really good that will not bear the test of a serious and solemn
reflection at the closing scene of life, when we shall view present
things in connection with Eternity. I have nothing specially
interesting to tell you respecting our domestic concerns. We
have had company with us almost the whole time since you left
us. Clarissa Fiske has been with us about two months; she
went home last Saturday. We now have (while I am writing to
you) Esquire Fiske's daughter, and Miss Hobbs with us on a
visit. Mr. Bennett has been unwell and confined to his chamber
for some days, but is getting better. Prof. N. W. Fiske preached
there last Sabbath. There has been a very serious awakening
and attention there of late; at one time about seventy-five under
some serious impressions, and were considered as enquirers.

I don't know how your mind has been exercised on those important subjects since you left here; but I cannot but entertain
a hope that the favorable situation you are in for reading good
books, and especially the Bible, with the useful instruction and
counsel which I hope you will gladly receive, will be blest to
lead you to a correct understanding of the sacred scriptures,
to the true character of God, to a deep and humbling sense of
our lost and fallen state by nature, the necessity of regeneration,
of the divine agency of the Holy Spirit to effect this change in
our hearts, and by his sanctifying influences to lead us to love
and embrace the precious Saviour, who so freely offers himself
to all those who will come to him and accept of him in the
way which is so plainly pointed out in the gracious promises of
the gospel. Don't, I entreat you, consider these things as
trifling concerns, that may or may not be worth your attention.
But, as you wish to obtain future happiness and avoid future and

eternal misery, strive to remember your Creator " in the days of your youth."

I must again urge upon you an industrious improvement of your time in a close application to your studies. You must realize that your very existence as a scholar depends very much on the proficiency you make in your present situation. It would give me more unhappiness to hear that you were growing careless and inattentive in your studies than it would to have you banished forever from college. I do hope that I shall never be called to this painful trial. Nothing but a determined resolution to exert yourself to the utmost of your abilities is necessary to make yourself respectable, useful, and happy, and a comfort to your parents and friends.

That you may thus improve the advantages which you are so highly favored with, and in your youth evidence not only an amiable outward deportment, but also a sincere and earnest solicitude to be led to the knowledge and belief of the truth and the way of salvation, through the atoning sacrifice of the precious Redeemer, shall be the unceasing prayer of your affectionate parent,

I. WARREN.

P.S.— I hope you will very soon give me some evidence of your industry and improvement, by writing to me a good, long and sensible letter, and give me some account of your studies, reading, etc.

N.B. — You will remember that I have always requested you to keep the letters which I write to you, and not let them be lost or destroyed.

CHARLESTOWN, March 28, 1827.

MY DEAR SON: — Although I have seen you since your letter of the 7th ult. came to hand, I think it may not be improper to make some remarks upon it. You observe that " all my letters are filled with good advice," and my endeavors to inspire you with ambition and to make you a PRIEST. It is true I wish you to be inspired with ambition, but not a vain, empty, selfish ambition, merely to make a show in the world, or to shine as a pompous literary character. But I do want, and I long to see you possess, a laudable ambition to be truly virtuous, amiable, and exemplary in your moral and religious deportment, and to strive more to be a really good and useful man than to be eminently great in the world.

The observation you make respecting the danger of injuring the health of students by a close application to studies is by no means correct. I believe there are ten students that destroy their health for want of proper attention to their diet, and want *of exercise*, to one that injures his health by too intense studies. I know it will be hard to convince you of this. But I have, myself, seen such evident demonstration of the fact, that I am not left to any uncertainty respecting the correctness of it.

In your remark about the choice of a profession you observe you " think it the best way to give yourself up to fortune and chance," etc. I do not wish you to be in haste about deciding on a profession at present; but I should have been much more pleased with the sentiment, if you had said " I shall give myself up to the wisdom and guidance of a kind, benevolent Providence." I have so frequently expressed to you my views of the importance of cultivating the mind, of forming early habits of industry, and improving the precious season of youth in the acquisition of a *useful* and *religious*, as well as a literary education, that I can scarcely say anything new on the subject. But I should not discharge the duty of a faithful parent without often bringing these things into your view. It would be nothing new if I tell you that I feel a great solicitude and concern for you that your time may be well occupied in not only laying a good foundation for a respectable standing in society, but, what is still more important, to be qualified for and possess a disposition to be extensively useful in promoting the welfare and happiness of your fellow-probationers for eternity; and in doing this, with a proper reliance on divine grace, you would greatly add to your own enjoyment.

Your six months' term has seemed to have passed away like a dream. I hope, however, it has not been lost, but that you have made some good and useful improvement of it, and that your mind is more consolidated and become nearer approximated to manhood and maturity of judgment and dignity of deportment, which even a youth is abundantly capable of acquiring, by one who possesses the great advantages which you enjoy, with a proper improvement of your time in reading, sober reflection, and the study of human nature.

I have been three times to Woburn within a few days, on the business of the contemplated academy. A number have united and bought forty acres of land, out of which there is to be appropriated a sufficient quantity for the establishment of the institution. There is now nearly the amount of the five thousand dollars subscribed. We were on the grounds yesterday to lay out the plan for the building.

The attention and revival at Woburn continues and daily increases. About two hundred attended the meeting of enquirers this week. It is not likely that there is much danger of so many of all ages becoming " *crazy.*"

There is a very general attention and much evidence of serious religious impressions with us in Charlestown.

I have delayed writing to you because I had not concluded about coming after you; but as the going is now pretty good, I have made up my mind to come in a chaise for you next Saturday, unless the weather should be very unfavorable. In that event you must come up on Monday morning in the stage.

Dr. Woods desires me to remember him affectionately to you. Present my regards to Dr. and Mrs. Storrs,

Affectionately yours,

ISAAC WARREN.

Mr. George W. Warren,
At Rev. Dr. C. M. Storrs',
Braintree, Mass.

SABBATH EVE.,
CHARLESTOWN, Aug. 2, 1829.

DEAR GEORGE: — I received your very short letter and intended writing to you before this time; but the almost constant
calls and cares of one kind and another, together with the
weakness of my eyes, seem to deprive me of the pleasure of
writing otherwise than on necessary business. It is gratifying
to me to learn that you are so well pleased with your employment, and, the more so, to hear that your services are so well
received. This, I hope, will have the good effect, now in your
first setting out, to add fresh stimulus to your exertions. And
now I feel impelled to breathe out an ardent wish, and I hope
a devout prayer to God, that, with this good beginning in your
present employment, you may be led to serious reflection and
an inclination to read and study the Bible with a deep interest
in what concerns your future and eternal happiness, that you
might feel your lost and ruined state by nature, and the need
you stand in of an interest in the atoning sacrifice of the blessed
Saviour and Redeemer. It is impossible for you to conceive
what joy this would give to me and all your pious friends, if
you would but be persuaded to make this a subject of serious,
thoughtful reflection, and earnestly beg of God, your Saviour
and Redeemer, to lead your mind to the knowledge of the
truth, and to embrace the precious promises in the gospel, —
especially to the young, — "Those that seek me early shall find
me." You may think there is no need of a change of heart,
and because others wholly neglect religion that you shall do
well enough without it; but, I beseech you, if you have any
regard for your aged parent and the happiness of your immortal soul, that you will not let the precious season of youth pass
away in a thoughtless unconcern upon the most of all important subject.

However your mind may be at present, I don't by any means
give up the hope that you will yet be inclined to the study of
Theology, and make yourself so eminent that you may some
future day be so abundantly useful to the Christian world, and
so qualified by literary attainments, that you may be called to

be a Professor in Cambridge University; and only think how much more agreeable this would be, than to be connected with the bar! I had infinitely rather see you an eloquent advocate for Christ and the salvation of precious souls than to see you the greatest orator that ever was known in Greece or Rome.

I am so desirous that you should be trained up for some great and important good in the world that I cannot be reconciled to the idea of your studying law, and want to have you keep your mind from inclining that way. If you can be persuaded to love and embrace religion, in your early youth, you would not be at a loss what profession to engage in. If you would make yourself as eminent for learning and piety as Dr. W.'s son how would it rejoice the hearts of your best friends!

I intended saying something to you by way of advice about your present situation and employment; but you are doing so well, perhaps you will think there is no need of it. I must, however, repeat what I have many times said to you, that now is the favorable time for you to form and establish a character for life, and you can (in your young and youthful days) hardly conceive how important it is that this character should be formed upon the basis of the purest principles of *strict morality*, with a dignified manly deportment, which should always be evident in the distinct *emphasis* and expression as well as cultivated style in conversation.

Although my advantages for education were very limited yet I have had many years of experience, and have gained some knowledge of the world and of human nature, I hope, therefore, that you will think my friendly and paternal advice worth your serious attention.

As you calculate to apply yourself (the coming year) pretty closely to your "digging," I must give you a word of advice about your health, your diet, and exercise. I wish you to be made sensible how important this is for your own enjoyment, as well as future prospects and usefulness in the world. How many young students have ruined and broken down a good constitution merely for want of resolution to keep up that daily exercise which is so necessary to preserve a good state of health! A careful attention also to your diet is of no small importance.

Do but exert yourself to conform to my advice, and it shall be my endeavor to comply with your wishes as far as may be consistent with your best good and happiness both here and hereafter.

From your affectionate parent,

ISAAC WARREN.

P.S. — Mr. Stowel's shop was broken open last night, and 'tis said four or five hundred dollars' value in watches and silver things stolen, — an unfortunate thing for him. There was one watch valued at sixty dollars. I hope it was not yours.

Mr. George W. Warren,
    Teacher at the Academy, Woburn.

My dear George: — The address that is presented to you in these lines is not intended to meet your eye until the hand that writes them shall be mouldering in the grave. You must, therefore, consider them as coming to you with all the compassionate and affectionate feelings of a dying parent, whose deep concern and great solicitude for your present and eternal welfare will forever lay near his heart. In the firmest hope that in what I address to you as my solemn and dying counsel and advice, I shall present such things as shall be considered by *you* as of the utmost importance for your serious reflections. As life is so very uncertain, and I know not how soon or suddenly I may be called to the bed of death, and when I endeavor to realize what my views and anxiety will be for you, in such a situation, there are so many things that crowd into my mind, and so many important subjects that I should want to give you my advice upon, that I hardly know how to begin or what to commence with. But, on a few moments' reflection, I feel it to be the most of all important to urge and press it upon you, as with my last and dying breath, to devote and give up yourself to God in your early youth, and to love and read with attention the precious truths contained in the sacred Scriptures. Oh, do not, in all your studies, neglect that precious book that is of infinitely more value than all other books in the whole universe! There you will find a full and faithful account of the creation, — the fall and redemption of sinful man. You will find that our first parents, though created in innocency, soon fell from that happy state and became obnoxious to the Divine displeasure, and that by nature we are all sinful and depraved creatures; but that early and precious promises were made to our first parent of a Redeemer, which should, in due time, come into the world. That the ceremonial law and the Old Testament prophecies pointed to a Saviour to come. And in all the sacred scriptures there are precious promises made to the returning sinner, and especially in the New Testament, where the Saviour is revealed as freely offering life and eternal salvation to all that are willing to accept of him as he is offered in the gospel. How many precious promises do we find in the word of God, and more particularly to the young! "Those that seek me early shall find me." This sentence is worthy to be written in letters of gold. It is enough to excite and encourage every youth who reads them, with the other precious promises in the word of God, to lay hold on that hope set before them in the gospel.

Whatever your circumstances shall be in this world, be sure to value and prize the sacred scriptures as your most inestimable treasures; and, whatever may be your employment or profession, never forget that you were born for an endless eternity, and that nothing short of vital, experimental religion can ever qualify you for real enjoyment in this world or permanent happiness in that world of glory beyond the grave.

Very few, if any, have greater advantages for acquiring a good education than what have fallen to your lot. Oh, let not these privileges be lost, or worse than lost, upon you! If you should live to acquire a public education, it is my most earnest, and, I hope, sincere prayer to God that your mind might be led by the divine agency of the Holy Spirit to the contemplation of the sacred scriptures, with a view to the study of theology. However volatile your childhood and youth may have been, I

believe there are others uniting with me in this ardent prayer
that your views and your heart may be changed; that you may
be led to see and feel the native depravity of your heart, and
the absolute need of a Divine and Almighty Saviour, and his
atoning sacrifice and perfect righteousness to be applied to your
soul, and that you may live to be qualified for and made the
happy instrument of proclaiming the glad tidings of salvation to
a lost and ruined world.   Whatever your present views of these
things are, I cannot but entertain a strong hope that the many
prayers that are offered up for you to your heavenly Father, to
your Divine Saviour and Redeemer, will, sooner or later, be
answered, and that you will be brought to love and accept of
the blessed and glorious display of divine grace so freely offered
and held up to view in the gospel of Christ.

The foregoing is principally on the important concerns of
religion, as it respects your present and future well-being; but
I have other and very interesting concerns to present to your
mind on the importance of cultivating an amiable disposition
and respectable standing in society.   This is of vast importance,
both as to your own enjoyment as well as extensive usefulness
in the world.   As to a good disposition you are acquainted
enough with human nature to know that, however pleased and
pleasant you may be generally, yet that you are, at times, subject to rather an impetuous and rash turn of mind.   Now, to
conquer this, and bring your mind *habitually* into a more mild,
easy, genteel, yet dignified deportment, both at home and
abroad, so as at all times to appear like a well-bred, sensible gentleman, as well as one deserving a literary character, must require no small exertion.

The acquisition of these qualities, together with good moral
virtues, must require a studious attention to books of general
reading as well as the classics, and a good deal of study of
moral philosophy and human nature.

Whatever profession or calling in life you may adopt I charge
you to be diligent, industrious, and strive to live, not for yourself only, but to be useful and do much good in the world, both
with your talents and property.   Don't, I entreat of you, imbibe this dangerous impression, that you have nothing to do

but to live away in an idle, useless manner of life, and thus spend what may come into your hands. I wish you to possess a kind, noble, and generous heart; but always guided by heavenly wisdom and good, sound judgment. As you value your own enjoyment, both here and in the future world, I charge you always to be kind and attentive to your *mother*, and thus endeavor to compensate her for all that she has done for you. I charge you to read this letter *frequently*. And may these solemn admonitions be deeply impressed on your heart, as coming from the dying lips of your affectionate parent,

ISAAC WARREN.

LETTERS

HAMPTON, N.H., May 19, 1823.

HONORABLE FATHER: — I now write a few lines to you. I confess that I have been guilty in cutting up two handkerchiefs. I will tell you the whole story: I tied two handkerchiefs around my waist so that I might run fast. I wanted it off, and could not untie. I took out my knife and cut it off. This is the whole story. Mr. Webster says that he is not satisfied unless you are. I am sorry that I did it. I hope that you will forgive me. Please to write to me by Major Lovering, which will always be answered by

Your affectionate son,

GEORGE WARREN.

[WRITTEN WHEN TEN YEARS OLD.]

FRAMINGHAM, January 26, 1824.

MY DEAR FATHER: — I will now write a few lines to you to inform you of my welfare and progress in my several studies. I have got most half-way through the Fifth book of Virgil's Æneid. I am reading about the sports which Æneas instituted at the grave of his father, on the first anniversary of his burial. The manner of showing respect for departed friends was very different then from what it is at the present time. We should think it strange enough and altogether improper for an only son like Æneas to call people together to have racing, boxing, and a shooting-match, at the grave of his father, meaning by these sports to show respect to the memory of his parent; but this was the case with the Trojan Æneas. They first tried their skill in managing vessels, to see which of the four could row a vessel to a certain rock in the sea and back again the quickest. The one who was victorious had his head bound with green laurel, and had a cloak woven with gold and ornamented with a border of purple. They then, for the second sport, tried to see which could run the fastest, and the one who beat received a handsome reward from Æneas. After this play was ended two distinguished champions engaged in boxing. One of them got almost killed. We should think this an extraordinary sport. After the two boxers were parted, and the victorious one had knocked down a bull with his fist, they had a shooting-match. Æneas had a mast fixed in the ground and a dove hung to it by a string. The first fired the arrow and struck the mast, the second cut the string and the dove flew, but it was brought down by the arrow of the third archer. Acestes, the king of Sicily fired the arrow up in the air, and it took fire and was consumed, and so he was named Victor, although he did not kill the dove for it was killed before. The fifth sport was a sham-fight by thirty-six boys on horseback. These things took place a great many years ago. For Æneas (so Mr. Pike says) lived about the time of Samson, three thousand years since. Virgil wrote this less than two thousand years since. I will not trouble you any farther at this time with my stories from Virgil. I continue my studies in history and arithmetic, etc. There are between forty and fifty scholars in the academy, — twenty-five of which board in Mr. Pike's family. The scholars in the school are attending to various studies. Some to natural philosophy and astronomy, which, from the remarks I hear made, I should think must be very interesting. Chemistry, algebra, surveying, also are studied, besides Latin and Greek, English grammar parsing, writing, etc.

I have written so much I fear that I shall exhaust your patience. I must close by subscribing myself ever

Your affectionate son,

GEORGE W. WARREN.

I have the pleasure to say to Mr. and Mrs. Warren that their son is very industrious, and behaves much to his credit.

With much respect your obedient servant,

A. W. PIKE.

FRAMINGHAM, April 28, 1824.

MY DEAR FATHER:—As I promised to write a letter to you in the course of a few days, I will begin to tell you concerning my situation and studies. It is only a few days since I wrote you before, so that I have not had much time for improvement. I have only reviewed the Bucolics, and I am now reviewing the Eighth Book of Æneid. In the Seventh Book it tells us that "Æneas, after many adventures and dangers on the ocean, arrived in Italy, where he was kindly received by Latinus, king of the Latins, who gave him his daughter Lavinia in marriage. Turnus, king of the Rutuli, was the first who opposed Æneas from his having long made pretensions to Lavinia himself. A bloody war ensued in which the Trojan hero was victorious, and Turnus slain. In consequence of this, Æneas built a city, which was called Lavinium, in honor of his wife Lavinia."

We are also reviewing Goldsmith's Roman History again. In the beginning of Goldsmith's there is an account of the birth of Romulus and Remus, which I think is very interesting. Without a knowledge of history,—especially Goldsmith's Roman History,—we lose a great part of Virgil. I like the study of Virgil and History very much. I am also attending to Geography and Colburn's Arithmetic. There will be an exhibition at the end of the term, which I think will be as good, if not better, than what they used to have at Hampton. I should like to see you here at that time, and you can carry me home. Vacation will be a fortnight from Friday. I shall be very glad to see mother up here this week.

I remain your affectionate son,

GEORGE W. WARREN.

MAY 14, 1824.

This letter would have been sent long since, but I heard that my mother was at Weston, passing some days, and Uncle Fiske told me she would visit at Framingham. You will therefore excuse me for not sending sooner, for it was written a fortnight since. The school is to be examined on next Wednesday. I fear that we shall not be prepared to act all the dialogues, which was expected; but if we do not on Thursday, as was intended, Mr. Pike thinks that it will be quite as well at the beginning of next quarter.

GEORGE WASHINGTON WARREN.

AMHERST COLLEGE, Aug. 11, 1827.

MY DEAR FATHER: — Again I have taken the liberty to write you, although I told you in my last letter that I thought I should not have time to write you another, and hoped that you would, therefore, give all due attention to the subject of the last; and that you would be persuaded, and soon would acquaint me of your consent. But I feared lest some other subject was under consideration in your mind, or that you might be induced by arguments, comparatively trifling and futile, to go on in the same course as at present, so that either through the want of consideration, and by not paying sufficient attention to the subject, the short remainder of this term would pass away, and I not obtain my object. Although I generally felt assured, and had the greatest confidence that this would not be the case, yet, not willing to run even the *smallest* chance of not obtaining my request (for I would rather be willing to hazard anything else than to have the least hazard of this, and would be willing to do anything practicable in order to obtain this one request), I thought that it would be best for me to use as much time as I could possibly spare in writing you another letter on this important subject. And did I suppose that you would not be persuaded, even with these two letters, I should not hesitate in writing to you many more; for there are arguments enough in

favor of this place which would well and profitably employ
numbers of letters on this subject. But I think this is not necessary to accomplish my object. For, if you had even the least
prejudice against this plan, it would not have to be my lot, in
order to remove them entirely, to endeavor to have you adopt
altogether new resolutions, and to take a new course, but it
would only be to induce you to renew your attachment, and to
put in force some plan to which I believe you have often been
strongly inclined. To induce yourself to this I think you would
only need to read over the letters that I wrote you on this subject last year, and there, and to think over the feelings and,
perhaps I might say, determinations, which have occurred to
you within the last nine months. If you do this, and if you
consider and reflect rightly, attentively, and without prejudice,
which I humbly hope and entreat that you will do, I cannot but
be confident that I shall obtain your free and willing consent.

But there is another subject to which I would direct your attention. Perhaps you may not be inclined to give your consent
to my removal, because you may think that you cannot take me
away from here unless you come up yourself, and that you do
not feel able to be at so much trouble, etc., as to be willing to
do this; so, on the *whole*, you may say you think I had better
stay. But I hope that by such trifling circumstances you will
not put off the important question concerning the expediency
of obtaining a better education. But it is not absolutely necessary that you should come up. It would be, indeed, very
pleasant to have you come up, if you should feel willing and
able. But, if you do not, I hope you will not defer taking me
away on this account; for you could send your letter to the
President, or rather to Professor Fiske, and request that he
would obtain of the President a dismission for me, and that he
would see to my things, etc. Yet it would be necessary that
the letter should be very decided as it regards my dismission,
so that Professor Fiske cannot but do as you request.

I will now say a few words concerning this subject just now
hinted at. I mean with regard to what Professor Fiske may
say concerning my removal. I do not know whether or not he
would object to my removal; but, judging from the opinions he

expressed last year, and from his naturally warm attachment to this college, etc., he may, I think, be unwilling that I should go away. But I think that neither he nor the rest of the faculty can have the slightest ground for complaint if I take a dismission. And I am inclined to think that they *would not* complain when they consider the circumstances of my case. I also would request that you would not go according to what other persons may say with regard to this subject. For instance, Mr. Bennett.[1] Although I think he is a man of much learning and talent, yet I think that his opinion on this subject cannot justly have much weight; for you are, I suppose, well aware that he says, often times, things too hastily and without consideration; and I have no doubt but that, as soon as he heard that you had thought of putting me at Cambridge, he would break out with long speeches, and would tell you that it was your duty to keep me here, and would say many things at random; whereas, if he would pay as much attention to it as I have, and let it be the subject of his constant consideration for three months, which I think I can say I have done, I am persuaded that he would be as much in favor of the plan as he is now against it. The case is, he thinks that Cambridge College is in as bad state as when he was there, and will not consider that they have altered their course of study and made it more useful, been more strict in their laws, and have more advantages, and changed for the better in many respects. He also thinks that Amherst *must* be a great place, and does not consider that it has many disadvantages. But I do not write these things that you may undervalue him in any way; but I would only beseech you that you would take these things into consideration, and judge yourself. I am confident that you will do that which is just, and will give your consent.

But it is necessary that you conclude soon, for it is very desirable that I take a dismission this term, so that, as the term commences at Cambridge directly after their commencement, which is only a fortnight from next Wednesday, I may enter there as soon as the term begins. You see that by going to Cambridge I lose a fortnight of vacation, besides the long vaca-

---

[1] Rev. Joseph Bennett, an Orthodox minister, settled at Woburn, who married his half-sister, Mary Lamson, a daughter of his mother's by her first husband.

tion they have directly before commencement; but this will be
no sacrifice if I obtain my request. But (to return) I hope
that, as you will probably receive this letter on Tuesday, you
will on that day write to me, and put it in the post-office next
mail; for I should wish to have you write if you should conclude to come up.

Only, father, think how pleasant it would be to you and to
me to have me at Cambridge; it will occasion both of us less
trouble, it will be so handy; you will know all about the college
affairs, my situation, and will have much more comfort than you
do now; and, more than all, I shall obtain a better education.
Besides, as I can reasonably expect to obtain from this college
a very good recommendation, shall be just, and no more than
well, fitted to enter one year advance, and can commence, in
fact, a new college life. This is my determination, if you grant
my request. Now, father, I do entreat of you to give me your
consent. I ask it of thee more earnestly than I ever did anything else whatever. And, although, as I said before, I was
very desirous to go last year, yet my desire now is more than
doubly greater than it was then. Then, after considering, I
found that there were a few things in the way of my going; but
now I can see my way through clear, and there appears to be
nothing to hinder except your consent, which I beg of you no
longer to withhold. Do not throw away these letters, and put
off considering on them till vacation, — for then it will be almost
too late, — nor consider them as a notion of mine. No, do not
refuse me that which I have considered for a long time, and the
more I think of it the more earnest it makes me to obtain it;
for I should be willing to part with anything else except with
this. But I cannot be brought to think that you will so much
disregard the wishes of your son as to refuse his greatest request, — a request, which if obtained, would not be the cause
of any evil, but, probably, of much good. If you grant me
this, you will ever have the thanks of your affectionate son,

GEORGE W. WARREN.

P.S. — I shall now employ what leisure I have this term in
looking at some of the Cambridge studies. I hope, father,

that you will be quick to send me a letter as soon as you receive this. This is certainly the last letter I shall write. I am in anxious expectation that I shall soon receive the good news that you have given your consent. Do not, I beseech you, — if you regard as anything my wishes, and, indeed, my welfare,— do not disappoint me.

Yours,

G. W. W.

AMHERST COLLEGE, Aug. 14, 1827.

DEAR FATHER: — I thought, when I wrote last, I should not write you again this term. But the faster the term is coming to an end the more earnest I feel to obtain my request. And being so very desirous and well convinced on my part, I could not refrain myself from writing you again so that you might not be wholly ignorant of my feelings on this subject. For I am persuaded, as I have repeatedly wrote, that, did you employ so much consideration as I have, and think and judge without prejudice, on the advantages that would be derived from my removal, you would not hesitate in the least, but would immediately comply with my request. With such feelings as these I cannot and you know I ought not to be silent, but to use my utmost exertions to have you give your undivided attention to the subject, and to constantly and fervently beseech you to comply with my request. This is what I think right and necessary for me to do, and with what I hope you will have no doubts to comply.

But it is time for me to close, as it is late, and the mail will soon be shut. I hope, father, that you will not in any way disappoint my favorable expectations; for I would rather be deprived of anything else; and I am well persuaded there will be nothing wanting on my part to make this removal extremely beneficial. I hope you will not be influenced by what some interested persons may say; they will try to have you believe that it would be injurious to me. But the ONLY way to determine is to TRY, and see. And I am willing to agree with you that, if you will put me there at Cambridge, and I do not answer all reasonable expectations, you may take me away and dispose of me as you choose. This is certainly doing everything in my power, and I hope *you* will not at all be backward.

I look forward with great pleasure to next week, when I expect to be preparing for Cambridge, and to entrust my instruction in hands of the most experienced teachers, and in an institution of best advantages. A disappointment of this expectation would be as bad to me as the denial of *any college* education. But it *does* seem that you will not occasion me this grief.

I hope that you will be sure to take me away this term, or else I shall lose considerable time. The time, you remember, is only about a week.

My dear father, it is in your power to bestow upon me the best of favors, and this, too, with but comparatively little trouble. The denial of this would be very grievous to me, but your consent of the same would (and greatly too) always be in the remembrance and gratitude of

Your affectionate son,

GEO. W. WARREN.

N.B. — I hope, dear father, that you will immediately send up here a letter containing a request for an immediate dismission, and I will always be grateful to you for the same.

I shall not write again, and expect this will be wholly sufficient.

GEO. W. W.

———

HARVARD UNIVERSITY, July 20, 1830.

This certifies that Mr. George W. Warren, who has now completed his course of study here, and is to receive his degree at the coming commencement, is a gentleman of good moral character, and competent, in my opinion, to instruct in all those departments of learning and science which are taught in our higher schools and academies.

SIDNEY WILLARD,

Professor in the University.

CAMBRIDGE, July 20, 1830.

This certifies that Mr. George W. Warren, a member of the Senior Class in Harvard College, has sustained a good moral character, and held a respectable rank as a scholar during the time of his connection with the college. He will receive the degree A.B., at the next commencement, and is believed by the bearer to be well qualified to take part in the instruction of the young in a school or academy.

HENRY WARE,
Prof. of Divinity in Harvard College.

NEW BEDFORD, March 1st, 1831.

MY DEAR FATHER : — It was not till the latter part of last week that Mr. Dix returned, and I received a letter from you. I am much obliged to you for the care you took to send me the books, which I found not in the least injured. I am sorry that I gave you so much uneasiness for not writing you so soon as you of right expected. I am fully sensible that I ought not to give you the least pain from that occasion, and I hope never to be found guilty again. The reason why I deferred answering you so long before was that I knew Mr. Dix was going soon, and I would wait to send by him. Will you (for I have one more commission) be kind enough to do up my " Shakespeare " and " Salmagundi " carefully in a bundle, and direct it to me by the stage which puts up at Shepard's, Bromfield street? I should like to have you send them as soon as you receive this.

What beautiful weather I have for my vacation ! If I had anticipated such a pleasant season I should certainly have made preparations to have gone home last Saturday ; but it is too late now to think of it. Twelve weeks will soon pass away again, when I shall have another week of leisure. Whenever you and mother can get ready to come I shall be extremely happy to see you, though you will not find me at Mrs. Waterman's, as I

am now at Mrs. Samson's for the present. Mrs. W. concluded
to give up boarding. There are a great many where I am now.
Mr. Dix is one. The house is crowded here, as is the case
with every boarding-house in town. Mr. Sanford thought some
of going to Boston. If he had he would have taken a letter
from me and called upon you. You would be much pleased
with him; he is an excellent school-master, — one who has married and settled upon it, so, of course, he likes the business.
Do send us some scholars. Why cannot Uncle Isaac send us
up his boy this next quarter? I have no doubt he would be
satisfied with his progress and the attention paid him here. I
cut out the advertisement we put in the paper here.

Oh! there is one more book that I want very much. It is
"Knapp's Lectures on American Literature." I lent it to
Hannah Childs a year ago. If you could get that, and send it
with the rest, I should be very thankful, though I am sorry to
trouble you with so many requests.

Allow me to renew my sincere thanks for the many marks of
affection and love you have shown me. Your last good letter
I have read over more than once, I assure you, and every time
I read it it strengthened my gratitude towards you, and made me
rejoice that I had a parent who, notwithstanding my many
faults and errors, still feels so warmly and tenderly for me. I beg
you never to think me ungrateful. I am sensible how much
I owe to both of you ever to entertain such a *thought*. I hope
I shall never think of you otherwise than with feelings of
respect and love.

You wish to know my motives—I mean my notions—of my
future profession, and I am bound to impart them to you,
though at present they are not very distinct and determinate.
You know, some time ago, I concluded *not* to be a physician;
then *not* to be a lawyer. On these two points I am as decided
as ever. I have tried school-keeping. I shall not live upon
that, though I like it for the while. Well then, what remains
but for me to be a parson? But I would not be one without I
could conscientiously, and unless I believed everything I
preached. As yet I know not what *doctrine* to believe, though
I do not much approve of preaching many doctrines, for I have

not yet made the Bible and theology my *serious study*, as I
intend to do. Yet it will be very uncertain whether the minister's life would suit me after all. I am sure the life of many
ministers would not. What would now take my fancy is a sort
of literary life. I should like to become a professor of some
kind in Harvard College, but such a place is not to be had
by me.

However, I hope I shall in some way do some good, and live
usefully and happily, for which I am confident I have the
prayers of my affectionate parents. I am glad to hear that
you have both been well. Mr. Sanford was sick for a week,
and I had the whole school to take care of. Accept my best
wishes and gratitude, and remember me kindly to all inquiring
friends.

Your affectionate son,

GEORGE.

NEW BEDFORD, March 20, 1831.

MY DEAR FATHER: — I was glad to hear from you on the
15th inst., especially as I had been anxiously expecting a letter
for two or three days before I had received your last. Be assured that it gave me great pleasure to read the letter, and I
could not but feel fortunate and grateful in having so high a
place in your affections and good wishes. I hope and believe
all feelings of love and affection are fully returned on my part;
and I consider it my chief duty now to cherish and promote in
my breast every possible respect and gratitude for my good
parents, who have both done and suffered much for me. I
hope you will not refrain from expressing to me your true feelings and sentiments through fear I shall not pay that regard and
consideration due to them. Believe me I shall always endeavor
to value whatever comes from you with as much veneration as
it is rightfully due to yourself from me. The contents of your
last letter were very gratifying, and I hope to receive many
more such, if you should have the leisure and inclination to

write them. At any rate I hope you will not harbor the least
doubt of the good reception of those that you do send.

I see you advise me to board with Dr. Holmes. But there
are many objections that put it out of the question entirely. I
like Dr. Holmes as a man, and shall visit him oftener; but
whenever I have called he has always seemed to be much engaged; in fact his society is very large, and I presume he
employs his whole time in attending to its concerns. I hope,
however, to get comfortably established ere long. By the time
you will probably come to see me — which I hope will be as
soon as you can find it convenient — I expect to change my
habitation once more, I hope for the last time in this town.

I am glad to be of your way of thinking as to a profession;
in truth I should delight to be a minister, could I be left to myself and to the convictions of my own understanding, unpreju-
diced altogether by others. But I feel I am not so at liberty.
I should not like to be a preacher of sentiments decidedly opposed to yours, and which you sincerely believe to be wrong;
nor should I like to engage in this profession with the promise
of disseminating doctrines the truth of which I might not be
persuaded of. So, with my present feelings, I should not feel I
was a *free* agent were I to follow the profession of divinity.
Though we may ever differ in doctrine, I believe I agree with
you as to the reality of piety and the necessity of a true religion.
I respect and love those who I think are Christians, — I
mean those who not merely *believe* in a Christian faith, but
who live and act according to the religion they profess. Such,
I believe, are found in *all* denominations, and I shall always
think so. Were I to be a minister I would unhesitatingly take
such ones for my example as young Henry Ware, Dr. Lowell,
and Mr. Dewey. Would you be contented to see me one of
such?

Should I follow a *literary* life, perhaps that *might* not support
me; would that make a difference with you, supposing I should
use all my exertions to improve my *mind and heart*, and endeavor to do good to all men? — which is the sincere and real
aim of my future plans, if I know my own mind. I should
like to have your full sentiments on these subjects.

I must now conclude with repeating my request to send me the books with one or two others; the whole I want are these: "Shakespeare," "Lectures on American Literature," "Salmagundi," "Crabb's Poems," "Dr. Channing's Works," "Classic Tales," and one volume of the "American Encyclopædia," which I lent to Mr. Marshall. Now, I do want all of these, and some of them immediately. If they are done up carefully, like the last bundle, and sent by the stage, they will reach here safely. Will you be kind enough to attend to it as soon as you can?

Remember me kindly to my dear mother and all friends.

Your affectionate son,
GEORGE.

NEW BEDFORD, Aug. 3, 1833.

MY DEAR FATHER: — It was both with pain and pleasure that I received your last. I felt the greatest pain when I discovered what your feelings were, and I own that I am conscious of deserving such expressions in a great measure. When you speak of the hardships and labor it cost you to earn your property, and of the sum that I have already cost you, and how long it took you to lay up that sum, I acknowledge that I had never before reflected upon it, and your remarks struck me forcibly; and the impression I received from this consideration, I promise you, shall have great weight upon my future conduct. I was pleased to find that the feelings of a father were still yearning for me; and this, with the hopes I cherish of doing better, and before many years of fully reëstablishing myself in your favor and confidence, are all that support me from despondency. Were it not for this I might wish not to live; but no, I am encouraged to live and I pray that my life may be spared until I have made glad the hearts of my parents and others dear to me, and until I have done something for the good of my fellow-creatures. You have read in the Bible of many pious men who even in their old age were grieved by the errors of their children, and yet the Lord converted them in answer to the prayers and patient well-doing of their fathers. And I, like the prodigal, would return to you for a blessing. The only way to make amends is to conduct better in the future. The property already spent upon me should be deducted from my future inheritance, and the little remaining, with good habits, may be to me better than the whole without the experience I now have.

In your last you enjoin upon me not to fully conclude upon leaving or remaining here; but for two or three weeks I had concluded that it would be better for me to remain; the reasons for it I will briefly state. In the first place, I could not, in honor or justice to the parents of my pupils, take myself away so suddenly, as some of them expect to send to me for years. I could not either dispose of my things here without making a sacrifice, as they were principally intended for a high school; and, if I should leave, there would not be an immediate succession to me, as the people here are averse to sending to strangers, and it takes quite a time for such to be established. A third reason is that I might consider myself as established here. Each term my school increases. I shall have more scholars next term than everbefore; and, if I should wish, I might remain here and do well for life, or until I should be offered some professorship; but, should I leave, it would be a loss of the time and money I have laid out in my present business. Besides, I have a growing love for school-teaching. I feel conscious I am doing some good; but, should I now change my situation or profession, it would be long before such prospects as I now have would open upon me. These are some of the reasons, and I hope you will excuse me for using my own judgment in what most particularly concerns my own welfare. My debts may be easily settled according to the calculation we made together. With regard to your coming, I hope the visit you next make to this place will happen at the middle of my term; coming at the close or beginning of my term does not have a good appearance, and, if it should happen so again, it would appear strangely.

Let me say one word about my own next visit at home. I hope that when you see me you will not constantly call in mind the expense and trouble I have caused, for then your reception will be cold and unpleasant; but look upon me as your only son and hope, — as one who is ready to confess his faults and would give you relief from anxiety, and by his future conduct would blot out all that is past; for, father, I have filial feelings ready to break out, if you would show in your manners and treatment a gentle and friendly spirit. For what is all this world to us? In a few years, compared with eternity, both of us will be laid in the dust; an age will pass, and we shall be forgotten on earth. Then, if our spirits should ponder upon what we at this time feel and act, how different will things appear! Then we shall wonder that we could have so conducted, we may, perhaps, regret that we were not more desirous of cherishing lively and sympathizing feelings of the filial and paternal kind; that we did not attend to the rule Christ gave on earth, that we should forgive *seventy times seven times.* But now we have an opportunity to prevent these unpleasant reflections in the future world; let us, while we live, be bound by free and true affection. I certainly am willing to come more than half way.

My vacation will be about three weeks, about half of which I shall spend in Stow. I should like to give Mary a long visit also, and I hope that we shall be in Woburn at the same time. I shall come home in a little more than a week after you have received this, — what day I cannot tell now.

Your affectionate son,

GEORGE.

NEW BEDFORD, Nov. 16, 1833.

DEAR FATHER: — I received your letter last Saturday. I have been putting off writing until it should be decided as to the time of my lecture. It has at last been decided that I should lecture on the Tuesday of Thanksgiving week. I have concluded to make a vacation at that time, in order to have my quarters correspond in future with the other schools. Of course I shall be prepared by the time, and I hope I shall be acceptable to you and the others. It will be pleasant to me to be at home at that time, and I expect much pleasure from my visit. With regard to my school, I have the same numbers that I had last term, though they are not quite enough; necessary expenses have increased, the price of board is greater, so I ought to be gaining more, and I hope to be able to do so.

Without caring too much for money, and setting my affections upon riches, I wish to learn to value it aright, and also I would desire and strive to know how to manage and use it properly. As I am approaching the age of legal freedom I feel it important, as you have often told me, to give this subject a more serious attention. Above all, I wish to form my plans for the future with a view to my own true welfare and the good of others. I hope that we may have an opportunity to converse upon these subjects, and I shall have one or two propositions or requests to make of you. Knowing that you wish sincerely for my true and everlasting happiness, I would willingly lay before you my plans and thoughts, and hope that we may enjoy sweet counsel and affectionate interviews.

With love to mother, believe me

Your affectionate son,

GEORGE.

LETTERS

FROM REV. JOSEPH AND MARY L. BENNETT.

WOBURN, Feb. 1st, 1823.

OUR DEAR BROTHER GEORGE:—We have long been anticipating the pleasure of writing you a few lines; but one thing after another has occurred to prevent. Your letter by mail was seasonably received, and afforded us much satisfaction. We rejoice in the consideration that you are placed in a situation so favorable to improvement in everything which can adorn your mind and polish your manners. We trust you are not insensible of the obligations you are under to that all-wise Disposer of events, who is permitting you to enjoy such distinguished privileges. You are not (like the majority of lads your age) compelled to labor for your daily bread, but located in a family where you are favored with the society of an eminent clergyman and a celebrated instructor, who are carefully watching over your daily improvements. Remember, dear brother, that of those to whom much is given, much will be required. At the last great day your advantages and improvement will be rigorously compared, and, if it shall then appear that you have not improved your time and your talents, your case will be awful; like the servant who knew his master's will and did it *not*, you will be "beaten with many stripes." Oh, do not disappoint your parents and friends, who are entertaining such high and pleasing expectations concerning you, by refusing to acquire that knowledge which alone can make you wise unto salvation! "Remember your Creator in the days of your youth." Consecrate to God the first of your fruits, the best of your days. Often think of the lessons of piety which your aged father has taught you. Let not a day pass without reading a portion in your Bible, — this is the best of books; in this you learn what you must do to be saved; in this, too, are laid before you the most excellent rules for the direction of all your conduct. Every morning and evening repeat the Lord's prayer, and try to understand at the time the meaning of every expression you utter. It is God alone who can preserve your life and continue to you the mercies you enjoy. Be kind and affectionate to your fellow-students, respectful and obedient to your instructor and the heads of the family in which you reside. Thus you will secure the friendship of your school-fellows, the approbation of your instructor, and the love of all with whom you have to do. Thus, too, you will cherish those amiable dispositions, and cultivate those correct habits which tend to conciliate affection and esteem in this world, and to promote that renewal in the divine image, which is indispensable to union with Christ in that which is to come.

Since you were here we have moved to Mrs. Reed's, and find ourselves well accommodated nearer the meeting-house. Mam. and Horatio spent a week with us just after we came here; and pa and mam. have been up to see us once since. They were well when we saw them last. We look forward with much pleasure to your vacation, and shall depend on your spending a part of it with us. We have only room to subscribe ourselves your affectionate brother and sister,

JOSEPH AND MARY L. BENNETT.

WOBURN, 1843.

MY DEAR BROTHER GEORGE: — Do you not recollect the time when I was a little girl of twelve, and you a little boy of two? I taught you the first hymn you ever learnt: —

> " My God permit me not to be
> A stranger to myself and thee;
> Amidst ten thousand thoughts I rove,
> Forgetful of my highest love."

How sweetly you used to lisp it out! Oh, how dearly I loved you! Thought you was a " nonesuch," and never should love any other child half as well. And then, sometimes, we would kneel down and say our little prayers together. Those times have all passed away, and a great many other pleasant hours have intervened.

And now you are a man of wealth and influence, and God has given you distinction among men. And you have it in your power to do much good in the world, and I trust you will have the grace to do it, and I know you have a benevolent heart.

Well now, for your sister. I have been a minister's wife, as you know; have seen some prosperity and some adversity; much sickness and some health; joys and trials mixed together. And now, in the prime of life, when our desire to live is as great as at *any* time, the destroyer has come; there is no mistaking his grasp; and I must leave dear home, friends, children; Mary without a mother; but it is all right; the Lord reigns, and does all things well. In Christ I am *happy; I can resign all.* On account of the difficulty of conversing, and knowing that *that* would *increase* instead of diminishing, I have written to most of my friends.

And now, my dear brother, will you permit a dying sister to address you? Will you accept my grateful acknowledgments for your many, *many* kindnesses? You have always been kind, both in sickness and in health; and have shown me many a favor, for which I feel truly grateful. You have always contributed to my happiness whenever we have been in each other's society, and I hope the same grace will prepare us both to

spend a happy eternity together. But it would rejoice my
heart, in the prospect of death, to know that your views of the
atonement were founded on those passages of scripture which
most plainly reveal to us the fact that the sufferings of Christ
on the cross were *vicarious;* I allude to such as these: "He
was wounded for our transgressions; he was bruised for our
iniquities, the chastisement of our peace was upon him, and by
his stripes *we* are healed." "He bears our own sins in his
own body on the tree." Here a decided efficacy is attached to
the death of Christ, as connected with the pardon of sin. But,
in order to make this atonement of any service to us, we must
feel that we are lost, for they that are *whole* need not a physician, but they that are *sick*. And we must go to Christ with
the feeling of utter helplessness, and casting ourselves at his
feet, by faith, lay hold "on the *only hope* set before us in the
gospel." This is not visionary, dear brother, but *real*. *I feel it
to be real,* — with eternity before me, and death at my elbow, I
know it to be real. And I rejoice that it is. I do not expect
to be saved on any other ground; here I started in the *beginning;* here I have rested, "Jesus Christ himself being the
chief corner-stone." And I have endeavored to show my faith
and love by serving this blessed God and Saviour. But not
one particle of dependence do I place on anything I have done
as a ground of acceptance before God. If you wish to know
the *foundation* of my hope of happiness, *Christ is all* and in *all;*
he is very *precious* to me in comforting and sustaining me under
extreme suffering. With the langour of disease oppressing my
system what should I do without an *Almighty* Saviour on
whom to lean? And now, my dear brother, are you on this
foundation? If not, I fear "*your house is built upon the sand.*"
"For other foundation can no man lay, than is laid, which is
Jesus Christ." "There is no other name under heaven whereby
we can be saved, than the name of Jesus Christ." If this Saviour is as precious to *you* as he is to *me,* then you are a *happy*
man; happy in life, and you will be happy in death. You will
be happy in resigning your earthly possessions at the call of
God; yea, and your *life* also. And you will be equally happy
in consecrating all your wealth and influence, life and health,

and everything to the service of Him who has bought you with his blood, redeemed and saved you.

Dear brother, I hope to meet you and all our dear family, and all our dear *families*, in one unbroken rank in Heaven. How *sweet* that *home* will be! We may well then sing, "Sweet home! sweet home!" Dear brother, farewell, *farewell!* May grace, *mercy*, and peace, be with you and yours, through time and eternity. So prays your *dying* sister. Amen and Amen!

MARY L. BENNETT.[1]

---

[1] A half sister, being the daughter of Isaac Lamson, and the wife of Rev. Joseph Bennett, of Woburn, who died, Feb. 11, 1843.

NOTE.— Mrs. Mary Lamson Bennett was a lady of great beauty and accomplishments. She might have excelled as an artist, as she both drew and painted with much skill.

Her pen was that of a ready writer, and for many years much of the poetry used on ordination and other public occasions, in Woburn, and the adjoining towns, was of her composition. Scores of stones in the town bear her epitaphs of her contribution. Her spiritual life was of rare depth and beauty. — *Lockport, N. Y. Journal.*

VALEDICTORY POEM.

DELIVERED BEFORE THE CLASS OF 1830, IN THE COLLEGE CHAPEL,
JULY 13, 1830, AT THE AGE OF 16.

WHAT glow of rapture thrills the youthful breast,
　　When free from school, in Harvard's buttons drest!
Past is the doom he feared so long before,
And all his anxious doubts and dreads are o'er;
With bounding step and grateful heart he wends,
And hears the long advice from troops of friends;
By them is warned, that " college is the worst
Of wicked places with temptations curst;
And no one can escape its vices clear
With goodly name and reputation dear,
Unless to closest study he withdraws,
Respects his tutors, and obeys the laws."
　Their minds imposed with many a righteous thrall,
Awake to every motion, every call,
The new-come Fresh as early cabbage green,
Around in gaping flocks are usual seen;
But should you chance with one alone to meet,
And with some notice should him kindly greet,
A thousand questions in exchange he asks,
Of old reports about, or tedious tasks;
If such a book is very hard to learn?
What study next and next will come in turn?
What direful punishment in danger lowers
O'er those who form in groups in study-hours?
If wandering spies are hired o'er us to look?
If all our sins are registered in book?

And if you think, he asks with fear appalled,
Before the Government he will be called,
Because one night, by dainty spirit led,
In Commons Hall he dared to toast his bread?

But 'tis not in the power of law or pain
The springy mind to cramp with tightened chain,
And Freshmen by degrees will surely learn,
That clubs will windows break — that hay will burn;
The tree of knowledge unto all is free,
And they in 'customed tricks will soon agree.
They soon begin to buy up ponies privy,
Next dare to tick their Grotius, then their Livy;
At last — should madness bear them on so far —
They'll keep a tick for Soda at the bar;
Until such mournful course of dissipation
Sadly defers their wished matriculation.

Now see the Sophomore with head up high,
And swinging arms, and bustling tread, sweep by.
What wonderful, surprising change is made
In him who has in college one year staid!
Could all so change, and never stop should come,
'Twould hasten on the bright Millennium.
None better puts to test than Sophic elf
The philo-sophic precept — " Know thyself;"
You'd think *that* knowledge, as you saw them pass,
They hourly sought of the reflecting glass;
With all its great importance well impressed,
In rich attire the subject they invest.

Now bold-faced grown when erst they showed them meek,
They venture e'en to interline their Greek;
At all restrictions they in silence sneer,
And nightly plot sly mischief far and near;
Their proudest deed they do in dark midnight
(When College is too poor her yard to light);
Bright bonfires blaze to shine each breakneck place;
But as Paul-prying proctors start the chase,
Discretion bids them drop their torch and flee,
And Sophic valor skulks behind the tree.

Nor think while schemes of frolic fill the head,
The mind is not through Learning's mazes led,
To hunt out crooked words in musty Lexicon,
To learn the alphabet round, square, or hexagon,
To translate signs and symbols into sense,
No skull so hard such work might not condense.
A novel task comes on, that comes with pain —
To con the *un*written labors of the brain,
Or search 'mid books or from what others deem
For hard-picked thoughts to feed a starving theme.
Such racking toil the unpractised wights deplore,
As each alternate week brings on the dreaded bore;
Nor less they fear the labored themes' return,
Whose fates made known what fitful passions burn!
Here curious Envy finds a meet resource,
On others' writing bends his chief discourse;
Or Disappointment hopes, with piteous sigh,
His theme *unparalleled* is yet marked high,
And would persuade, as his own case would suit,
That Style or Sentiment gains most repute.
    Of grave, sedate aspect the Junior walks,
Inured to thought, and seldom vainly talks;
Frequent reports, or cold neglect of mates,
Have keenly made him feel his rash mistakes;
Good sense instilled has softened down his airs,
Some worthy plan he takes — child's play forswears;
Save who a palm for punning luckless sought —
That itch is rarely cured when once 'tis caught.
Where naught but wild-grown weeds you late could scan,
Spring forth the ripening plants that form the man.
Now are the studies changed to sterner hue,
As Greek and Latin lore retire from view.
Arch Paley first lays moral science down;
Next ancient Butler, then word-piling Brown,
And modest Stewart, each in terms refined,
Do well to bother and confirm the mind.
Forensics, too, the growth of reason aid,
Or prompt to steal from books what Locke has said;

Though questions queer the wights are put to think,
On either side they bravely spread their ink.

    Thus far advanced our course, when cordial cheer
Burst forth as Harvard's troubled sky shone clear,
And Learning's temples brightened up to see
Glad tokens of a joyous jubilee;
Long may succeeding years resound with praise,
A just reward to proofs of better days;
Although too late our hapless ways to guide,
We well rejoiced when Harvard saw her Pride.

    At last we reached the summit of desire,
That height to which all college wights aspire,
Where rarely roused by bells they may enjoy
And their own time at their own wills employ.
Some slept — some smoked — some strode in dresses gay,
The passing wonders of the passing day;
And none found chafed the smoothness of their way,
Save who of modern tongues had ta'en too much;
Unhappy he who had to deal in Dutch!
Save when a *miss* the truants would contrive,
And grumbled all that one should grow to five.

    To skip in silence were a shame to me
The notice, Mathematics, due to thee;
Or Physics, — if thou should'st prefer that name,
Which all will ready give, nor doubt thy claim.
Oft have we sat, thy Master Spirit fearing,
As for a victim round his eyes were leering,
While we by books and hats from view would screen,
And silent mark a neighbor's dying scene;
Or when — for all his bulwark would defend —
One had to rise and risk his latter end,
With knowing show he'd blunder out a guess,
Or dumb — was doomed to *copy* more or less.
We all can part from thee with unwet eye
Most potent puzzler, unpoetic, dry!
If e'er again I venture thee my pate,
Dismal must be the need, or fair the bait;
As long as other ways to honor run,
Throw Physics to the Digs — for I'll have none.

Classmates, — thus like a morning dream have sped
Time's rolling circles round the reckless head;
And not a day, but some new impulse brought,
And not an hour, but with fresh feelings fraught;
Short time ago and we first met to gaze
On classic scenes with trembling and amaze;
And now our parting day will soon be o'er,
And we must say the words we've heard before.
Soon coming years may see us homeward tied,
'Mid household plagues, and pretty wife aside,
Threading a way with strange employments rife,
Through all the numerous nets and snarls of life.
Some may in busy, burly noise engage,
And search for fame to meet advancing age;
While some a still and social life will choose,
And with no comforts cross but moderate use;
Some may the Master's royal rod prefer,
And be such tyrants as their tutors were;
Others through foreign climes would like to range,
And seek in roaming round for cheering change.
    'Twere curious now to know, in youth's gay spring,
What various fare our future years shall bring;
Why may not then our several tastes betray
Our different lots which time will soon display?
Those we have seen disputing every day
How things should be, and doubting what you say,
Lawyers will turn, who must at aught connive,
And will on flaws and suits and quibbles thrive.
But should some one with longer tongue than head
Prefer to rule than wisely to be led,
He'll find it well to take the people's cause,
Cry, " They should govern, they should make the laws;"
Mayhap the people roused might take it ill —
An office fat confer to keep him still.
Then will loud plaudits to his honor rise;
Then will fame's breezes waft him to the skies;
Until, as upstart candidates complain,
The next rotation turns him out again.

But they, whose faithful habits, here instilled,
Shall lead them on in legal science skilled,
Will find that patience will reward them yet,
And gain the laurels labor e'er will get.
So we shall say — some future time, inclined
To know the stations our old classmates find,
And 'mong the rest, learn one's become a Judge,
A bookish scholar and laborious drudge, —
" We always thought that post would be his lot;
On College questions ne'er screwed he on *what is what.*"
    And we have those who always have shown forth
A genuine nature, and a modest worth,
Whose hearts are of the kinder feelings made,
Whose tastes and talent court the silent shade,
Whose greatest care is never to offend,
Whose best delight sweet converse with a friend;
These will be Parsons, who at the altar's shrine
Will suit their souls to thoughts and acts divine;
And placed o'er erring men their ways to guide,
All petty passions and low wants subside;
Content with generous deeds and lowly care,
Their sole desire what duty bids to dare;
And such will sure be happy, if their zeal
Dissociate not and make them sullen feel;
If from the world's disputes they keep them free,
Nor break their brains o'er hidden mystery.
They should be free as is their Maker's love,
Uncurbed by sects, all stirring strife above;
They should be calm, as better suits their trust;
Like goodly men who watch the way to dust;
Their aim should be to rear the opening mind,
To settle social peace among mankind;
Then they will live — the meed their worth repays —
As honored patriarchs of ancient days;
And die in peaceful and protracted rest,
By no one blamed, but oft by many blest.
    The Doctor's life has, too, its charms for some,
Who deem it sure — as to the choice they come —

An easy way to comfort and renown
To mix up drugs and drive about the town;
But ah! in their fond dreams they little know
The griefs and groans they'll have to undergo.
They've thought it hard enough to scud to prayers
When the knell dies before they reach the stairs,
Long after Sol has rose; but 'tis their doom
To doubt each moment's rest, each stay from home.
In the dead night all cold and dark, when sleep
Has just crept through the limbs, which senseless reap
The long-delayed repose — a knock is heard —
Another louder yet — and then a third;
At last the Doctor rouses — listless leaves
The snug embrace of well-tucked clothes — he heaves
A cordial sigh, then shivers in the squall,
And finds that now he five miles off must *call.*
Then quick prepares he to the aid be gone,
His hurrying chaise then swiftly rattles on,
Now mounts the hill, now sweeps the shortening plain,
Dashes down dale and steep, through crook and lane,
To where the alarmed house is all awake —
Their darling boy had got the stomach-ache!
    They too will have to hear the horrid yells
Of feeble veterans, or peevish belles,
Whene'er administered the noisome stuff,
Which ere they taste, they sing out, " Hold, enough! "
Or as a tooth is pulled with hand alert,
Resound their deafening screams, " You hurt! you hurt! "
Such screams are shrieks, as might remembrance crave,
Of *our* most dread and medical conclave,
How well we'd imitate the death-like moan,
As oft our Præses bid, " Groan, Doctors, groan! "
    Then there are times of wail and woe, that oft
Require a gentle care, a treatment soft,
When frighted souls are gathered in a room
To see a faithful friend await his doom,
And all in silence gaze with tearful eye,
Save one who asks you, " Doctor, must he die? "

Hard fate is set for those this art commands,
The hopes of many hearts are in their hands,
And while their skill and pains are finely shown,
Some tender feeling may they also own.
   Yet will not all a poor profession take,
Some may incline to know their comfort's sake,
Make it their aim to follow out their ease,
And plan their time and money as they please.
Such will discover ere much time ensue,
The misery of having naught to do;
The soul soon sickens — life a burden seems,
When days and nights bring only restless dreams.
Some constant clew to action we must choose,
One that is worthy, too, else toil we lose.
The lovely exquisite — in College known —
Whose care that best his person may be shown,
Who studies how to fix his varying phiz,
By twisted accents how all men to " quiz,"
To well disguise the inroads of a blow,
Or make his whiskers more luxuriant grow, —
Such one may haply force a transient smile,
Or catch a passing gaze but for a while ;
New tricks of oddness soon become the rage,
New beaux appear to turn the fickle age,
To whose new patent charms he quits his claim,
Himself retires — a proverb of his name.
A life thus barren leads the sensual wight,
Who wastes his days for what he dreams delight ;
Excess soon palls his pleasures — and a drone,
He drags his weary load unhelped and lone.
Who would not dread his vigor's bloom to pass
In drinking wine and looking in the glass?
Without a decent end for which to live,
One self-earnt praise to gild his memory with.
Better than bear the doom of such a lot,
To live aside unknowing and forgot,
And there unlearn whate'er was learnt before,
Or plod for ever 'mid confounding lore.

Now is the crisis that decides our fate;
Shall we arrive to crowning merit's state,
Or live like menials, and like misers die?
These answers in our future efforts lie;
Let none complain no anxious *part* is theirs,
That of no costly *deturs* they were heirs;
Not always do the world's fair favors run
To those who have most College honors won;
These things are oft in after years reversed
And some who here were last are now the first.
But if Remorse speaks out for time misspent,
If lost advantage bids you now relent,
'Twill be a hint to mark each present hour,
And teach you well to do while is the power.

How fondly do we cling, in sorry cheer,
Around the place so many bonds endear!
The thought of parting makes our bosoms thrill;
With all her faults, we love Old Harvard still;
These pleasant walks, this hallowed air around,
Our long attachments to these buildings bound,
Past hours of toil, our teachers' faithful care,
Rush in to lay our child-like feelings bare.
What jovial times we've had! which, though forbid,
Seemed more a pleasure as from strictures hid.
And oft in Friendship's season, when relaxed
We cast aside the pressing duties taxed,
How rioted our souls in gladdening fun!
And with delight the moments rapid spun;
While rung the rooms with many a peal and long,
As past the merry joke or choral song.
To us these days are o'er, but leave a spell,
That round their fame reflecting years shall dwell.
Gone is our boyhood — but through life attends
The grateful blessing of enduring friends.
And as this solace now we gladly view,
With willing hearts we leave our last adieu.

Adieu! Adieu! Old college days
   Have slipt from us forever;
The smiling world now spreads its ways,
   And makes us glad to sever;
Our breasts, rejoiced that they are free,
   With happy visions swell;
Good-by to tasks and commons' tea, —
   Old college times, farewell!

A few short weeks, and we shall go
   To scatter o'er the earth:
With our degrees and what we know,
   We hail our manhood's birth.
No more in this familiar cell
   On Sundays may we drowse;
No more can yon prayer-going bell
   From morning slumbers rouse.

A change comes o'er our prospects now,
   And we must change with them;
Before the Public we must bow,
   And act, lest they condemn;
A manly air and mien we need
   To match the rival throng;
For goodly name and lofty deed
   Should now to us belong.

Why should we sorrow or complain
   Of mixing with the crowd?
Or see upon the wide world's main
   But the impending cloud?
With merry heart and steady hand
   Let's widely stretch the sail,
And sternly keep a brave command,
   Like Cæsar in the gale.

Where'er we go, however dealt
　By fortune or by fame,
Oh may those ties be ever felt
　That Old Acquaintance claim; —
A classmate's name we'll oft repeat
　O'er cups of Friendship's wine;
A classmate's hand we'll kindly greet
　For sake of Auld Lang Syne.

Fair be our portions, and our lots
　For many a prosperous year;
Well may we live on favored spots,
　To friends and country dear. —
At last — may Hymen cross our ways,
　And happy couples cast:
Then be the remnant of our days
　As pleasant as the past.

ODE

COMPOSED AND SUNG ON THE CELEBRATION OF THE ANNIVERSARY OF
AMERICAN INDEPENDENCE, JULY 4, 1831, AT NEW BEDFORD, AND
SUNG IN BOSTON, JULY 4, 1881, WHEN THE AUTHOR WAS ORATOR OF
THE DAY.

SURVEY the wide-spread land,
  And tell us where on earth
There may be found a better band,
  Of more ennobling birth
Than they who breathe this liberal air,
And all its blessed influence share.

We pass the joyous days
  In liberty and love ;
As free-born men, we lead our ways
  Stern slavery above ;
Each can enjoy his lawful own,
His private thoughts, his social home.

No royal hand points out
  The way that we shall go ;
Oppression here builds no redoubt,
  In guise of friend or foe ;
But Freedom's soul, and Freedom's might,
Commands our land, — upholds our right.

'Tis Liberty's own soil ;
  Our fathers made it free
From savage waste, from foreign spoil,
  A patriot land to be ;
They hither fled in peace to live,
Here fought their sons that boon to give.

In stubborn strife 'gainst wrong,
    Our blessings they secured;
Through troubled times, through labors long,
    They faithfully endured,
Ere they could firmly fix their stand,
And form a fair, unfettered band.

Praise be their well-earned meed,
    The praise of freeborn souls;
As long as fame of lofty deed
    Down years unnumbered rolls,
America! for thee is won
Glory by many a noble son.

For those who struggle now,
    Far, far, beyond the sea,
God of our land! to Thee we bow,
    Oh! grant them victory;
Give them the spirit of our sires,
To strive for right till life expires.

NATIONAL HYMN.

FROM old Bunker's granite pile
 To bright Rio Grande's plain;
From Manhattan's glorious isle
 To Francisco's golden main,
Should rebel force or foreign arm
Disturb our peace or threaten harm, —
  Sons of Sires, who freed this land,
  Joined the States in union grand, —
  Stand like them in *their* good fight;
  Strike for Liberty and Right.

CHORUS.— Sons of Sires, etc.

Well our Fathers planned the scheme,
 Independence to declare,
Man from thraldom to redeem,
 Blessings glorious to share;
Their Faith the " Stars and Stripes " unfurled,
Best hope of Freedom through the world.

Then, with loyal heart and hand,
 Well we'll guard what they have won;
Those to whom we give command
 Must be like great Washington;
Our country o'er, — on every sea,
Our Flag shall tell that we are free.

When grim Discord holds the sway,
  When Ambition rules the hour,
When in battle's fierce array
  Foes assail; when dangers lower,
By noble deeds of former days,
By Lexington, and Yorktown's praise.

God preserve the President,
  Shield his honored path from ill;
Give the nation peace — content,
  Soul to do thy mighty will;
And *here* — from sea to sea shall be
The happy home of Liberty.

TO JAMES WALKER, S.T.D., LL.D.,

ON HIS 80TH BIRTHDAY.

TO thee, great Preacher of our youthful days,
   The Sage Instructor of our sons and sires,—
Whose holy life transcends all vulgar praise,—
   We send our offering grateful love inspires.

Not often does it fall to lot of man
   To live the term of threescore years and ten;
But fourscore years is now thy lengthened span,
   While FAITH'S bright visions glow within thy ken.

WISDOM has ever crowned thine upward path;
   Kind Providence has richly blessed thy store,
And much of GRACE and TRUTH thy life's work hath,
   Whose finest fruits shall still abound the more.

When our blessed Lord shall in his glory come,
   The world's great Harvest will be garnered up,
And thou revered wilt reach thy Heavenly home
   Bearing thy sheaves and drinking of his cup.

AUGUST 16, 1874.

GOVERNOR WINTHROP'S RETURN TO BOSTON.

AN INTERVIEW WITH A GREAT CHARACTER.

A POEM READ AT A SOCIAL MEETING OF FIRST CHURCH, AND ALSO AT THE
THURSDAY EVENING CLUB, MARCH 25, APRIL 20, 1882.

ON the seventeenth day of September, A.D. 1880, the two
hundred and fiftieth anniversary of the foundation of the
town of Boston, the event was commemorated, among
other ways, by the inauguration of the statue of John Winthrop,
in Scollay Square. He is represented by the renowned sculptor in
the garb of a gentleman of his day, holding in his hand the royal
charter of the Massachusetts Colony, which he brought over with
him.

His serene countenance falls like a benediction upon this city of
ours, which shows a wonderful and prosperous growth. He may
be said to be the founder of the First Church of Boston, of the City
itself, and of this Christian Commonwealth, — a threefold distinction. To have been the founder of a single one of these would
have insured his immortal fame.

He was also the author of the covenant of the First Church,
which was gathered in Charlestown, Aug. 27, 1630, and which
soon after removed to the Boston side of Charles River. The
covenant is in these words : —

" In the name of our Lord Jesus Christ, and in obedience to His
holy and divine ordinance, —

" We, whose names are hereunder written, being by His most
wise and good providence brought together into this part of
America, in the Bay of Massachusetts, and desirous to unite ourselves into one congregation or church, under the Lord Jesus
Christ, our Head, in such sort as becometh all those whom He

hath redeemed and sanctified to Himself, do hereby solemnly and religiously (as in His most holy presence) promise and bind ourselves to walk in all our ways according to the rule of the Gospel and in all sincere conformity to His holy ordinances, and in mutual love and respect, each to other, so near as God shall give us grace."

Probably there are very few, if any, original documents in America of so ancient a date which have been preserved, and which are still in force, as this identical covenant, which has been signed and kept by hundreds in each generation for nearly three centuries. Far superior to the Andover creed, or to any other creed of seminary, council, or church, it has ever been a bond of union, and not a bone of contention. Aptly phrased, and including all the essential conditions of a vital church organization, it will stand for centuries to come, and will outlast all creeds of human invention, ever promoting beneficence and charity.

This poem represents the spirit of Governor Winthrop returning to the city and the capital of the Christian Commonwealth he had founded, and taking possession of the bodily form which the artist has reproduced of him, clothed in his own antique costume. He surveys the extended limits of Boston, including Charlestown, with Bunker Hill Monument, and four other townships with hundreds of church steeples pointing to the sky. He misses from the old site on Cornhill the single house of worship where Wilson and Cotton preached, and where he was wont to expound; but soon he descries from afar, in his mind's eye, standing where, in his time, the waves of the sea were surging, the beautiful church edifice and the elegant chapel where five hundred Sunday-scholars are weekly taught. He dwells with supreme satisfaction upon the good deeds done by the church he established, and predicts for it a still more prosperous future and a greater spiritual growth. He recognizes only two things which existed in his day, and have remained unchanged, — the church covenant he wrote, as it were, by inspiration, or at least by a wise forecast of future needs, and the Communion cup he gave, which has singularly escaped the hazards of fire and the chances of time, and which has been, ever since, constantly used in the holy commemorative service.

Upon these almost universal changes he makes some appropriate reflections. To " sit in the stocks " was a punishment commonly imposed in his time for various offences. Richard Frothingham, in his " History of Charlestown," gives a view of the stocks that were set in the market-place with this mode of punishment applied. The view is here reproduced. " It was much used," says Frothingham,

" and several times repaired. A sentence by the selectmen for ' drinking to excess.' shows that one hour's sitting in the stocks could be compromised by paying 3s. 4d. money.". Winthrop, of course, would be struck with the different use of the word now so frequently spoken. From the fact that all investments of his day are swept out of existence, he predicts that the properties now held as most secure and reliable will in as long a time disappear. He illustrates the superiority of man, in his own best estate, to all wordly possessions.

His allusion to the vision of Rev. John Wilson, the first minister of the church, recalls the following passage in his diary, as quoted by Hon. Robert C. Winthrop in his " Life and Letters of John Winthrop." vol. 2, page 108.

" The pastor of Boston, Mr. Wilson, a very sincere, holy man, . . . told the governour that before he was resolved to come into this country, he dreamed he was here, and that he saw a church arise out of the earth, which grew up and became a marvellous goodly church."

The present church edifice well answers this description ; built with exquisite taste after a most appropriate design, and bearing the palm of all the costly churches in the new part of Boston for fitness, beauty, and permanency.

The Thursday Lecture, which was the special clerical and social occasion of his time, he finds abolished ; and he observes that the Thursday Evening Club is now a characteristic feature of Boston. This was formed for social, scientific, and literary objects. Among its founders and early members were Edward Everett, a member of First Church, and Hon. Robert C. Winthrop, the distinguished descendant and representative of the Winthrop family. The one referred to in this interview as the then leader of the Club was its late President, William B. Rogers. He was a man of superior scientific attainments, with a power of apt expression and a felicity and fluency of utterance indeed remarkable. By his efforts and influence the Massachusetts Institute of Technology was established, —a lasting monument of his zeal for technical science the most needed factor in popular education. In making an address to the Institute at its commencement exercises, May 30, 1882, he was struck with death ; he left the very place of his heart's and life's devotion for the spirit-land of Winthrop. His predecessors in the office of President of the Club were John C. Warren, the nephew of General Joseph Warren, Edward Everett, J. Mason Warren, and Bishop Manton Eastburn. The historic mantle of the office has now been cast on Colonel Theodore Lyman, upon whose well-stored and lofty head honors have fallen thick, but no faster than merited.

Josiah Quincy the elder, the second on the roll of Boston's distinguished Mayors, declared that the city might well adopt Winthrop as its patron saint. His was an ideal, saintly life, and his character, in a sense, supernatural. He bore success and defeat in a political election with like equanimity, — a trait that, as it were, by a law of heredity marks with special honor his living representative. Whether in office or out, and possessing large estates or, one after another, deprived of them, he kept his mind active and his brain industriously working for the development of a higher social life under Christian culture in a virgin land, by his leadership, under the Providence he devoutly acknowledged, to be fitted and fashioned for a new and powerful country, of which Boston was to be a memorable city.

Nor could he fail to remark upon the location of the statue set up in his honor in Scollay Square, rather than on Boston Common, which he had laid out and secured to posterity. The City Square in Charlestown, where he first unrolled the old charter of the Colony before the new government at its first meeting here, would have been a better site for it than the one selected.

Difficult it is, indeed, to set down in worthy lines the remembrance of the interview herein depicted. Of course it has been faintly and inadequately done. Let us hope, however, that, should Winthrop's spirit, two or three centuries hence, visit again the last and most eventful scenes of his earthly life, he will find Boston, though changed anew, yet vastly improved, keeping pace with all developments for the good of an ever-advancing race, and second to none in the Commonwealth or nation in true excellence and progress.

POEM.

There was a quiet hour in Scollay Square;
The cars and teams were blocked from getting there;
No longer shone the famed electric light, —
It flickered out and left the darkest night.
I seemed to feel a shock upon my arm,
And hear the statue speak: " I'll do no harm, —
An elder of First Church I think you are;
I have a message for you; come, prepare."

" Winthrop ! " cried I, " my venerable sire !
Do you reanimate your rich attire ?
Most glad am I to have this interview ;
Pray, tell me all you wish, things old and new."
" My friend," said he, " no ven'rable am I,
For mortals grow no older when they die ;
E'er since my earthly race I long have run,
My age has numbered only sixty-one.
Years are not counted on the heavenly shore,
For in eternal life time is no more.
The children sweet, the lovely bride forsooth,
Transferred, preserve the freshness of their youth.
Those who departed later are not found
Far to transcend them in their endless round.
More of the spirits' life I may not tell ;
Enough to say that with them all is well ;
God's universe has boundless worlds to show ;
His works will take eternity to know.

" But I would speak of your millennial time
Whose fame has gone through yon celestial clime.
Almost one seventh of the years our Lord
Has named for him, First Church has preached his word.
Its simple cov'nant ever served its need ;
It learned to live without a cumbrous creed.
Its ' goodly church,' fast built where flowed the tide,
Fulfils the vision Wilson saw with pride.
Its charming chapel opens wide the door
To the bright children of the suffering poor.
Ah ! blest are they who use for them their might !
Angels will bear them on their upward flight ;
And, in return the grateful youth will come,
With prosperous hands, to deck their Christian home.
The seed, wide-spread, will take its deepest root,
And, watered oft, will yield its tenfold fruit.
Erelong those hallowed walls will scarce contain
Those who shall flock to learn the precepts plain.

More week-day services will be required,
To hear the word by holy men inspired ;
And long shall those enduring arches ring
With pulpit tones, and songs the choir will sing.

" The cup I gave, and which you pass around,
The sole familiar thing about this ground,
Will prove a token true from age to age, —
May its partakers gild the sacred page !
" Oft as my after-knowledge takes wide range,
I note how wonderful the constant change :
No coin we used is current here to-day ;
The bills we passed you would not take for pay.
Our money funds required no 'safety' locks,
And differs much what we and you call ' stocks ;'
Men often find yours quite a dangerous game,
And get their foot stuck in them just the same.

" The Thursday Lecture yields no more its grace ;
Your Thursday Evening Club now takes its place.
The buildings strong we built have ceased to be.
Lands now most valued then were in the sea.
And so, few centuries hence, 'twill be again :
What now is property will sink like rain ;
Your mills, railroads, and bonds will be out-played ;
Then, too, your fruitful Calumet may fade.
Amass as much as one can call his own,
By right use only can its good be shown ;
Pile worldly goods in a superfluous whole,
They are not worth e'en one immortal soul.

" 'Twas not my lot to have large sums in store,
My wealth was gone ere mortal life was o'er ;
But Faith and Liberty I most did prize, —
On those twin rocks I bade a nation rise.
There was another John, you understand ;
He founded Learning's halls in this new land.

Not Vanderbilt, nor any moneyed name
Will e'er outshine John Harvard's brilliant fame.
Learn this: strive not for wealth that will not last,
But let your treasures be in Heaven cast;
These are alone the real things to crave.
While that will mould, like bodies in the grave.
Material forms to meet decay are sure;
The mind and spirit only will endure.
Hope's blissful visions, with its longings strong,
The will's high purpose, freed from thought of wrong,
Fond memory of good deeds that here were done,
Of sinners from their evil courses won,
The love and knowledge of the God Supreme,
Of Christ who came the fallen to redeem, —
These are, indeed, the good, substantial things
To which the soul for endless ages clings.

" Could I have marked where should this statue stand,
I would have placed it on that Common land,
Of past and coming times the great delight, —
With First Church spire and Capitol in sight;
My figure there should front the setting sun;
That, in review of any good I've done
During the last score years I passed on earth,
Posterity may better know my worth.

" I love the grand First Church, I love the State.
I planted both. Their growth through God, is great,
And both will flourish ever, while the sun
His circuit round this globe shall seem to run.
May every good St. Botolph's town betide,
And Thursday Club, led by the wisest Guide."

Of what he said, this is, condensed, the sum.
Then flashed the light; on came the busy hum;
Then Winthrop's spirit soared up to the stars;
Mute stood his statue 'mid the noisy cars.